BIG SKY

HEART

Allison O'Shea

Copyright © 2017 by Allison O'Shea.

www.allisonoshea.com

Publisher's Note: This is a work of fiction. Names, characters, places, and incidents are a product of the author's imagination. Locales and public names are sometimes used for atmospheric purposes. Any resemblance to actual people, living or dead, or to businesses, companies, events, institutions, or locales is completely coincidental.

Book Layout ©2017 BookDesignTemplates.com
Ebook Cover Design by www.ebooklaunch.com

Big Sky Heart/ Allison O'Shea. -- 1st ed.
ISBN 978-0-9996568-0-8

For my sister, Melissa,
who always follows her heart.

CHAPTER 1

"I wish I could love you enough for the both of us."

Emma heard the desperation in her voice, a choke barely above a whisper, and it only made her feel more pathetic. From the couch, she looked up at Blake's back and wiped the tears from her cheeks.

Blake glanced back, and unlike hers, his eyes were dry. His pile of suitcases in the center of the living room stood like statues in a field, monuments to the end of their relationship. Blake looked at his watch, then walked back into the bedroom and came back with a pile of shirts that he jammed into the top of one of the suitcases. He checked his watch again, and Emma wondered what it was he was running so late for.

"The apartment is paid up until the end of the month. If you want to stay beyond that, just let the landlord know and she can rewrite the lease for just you."

"Just me," Emma whispered.

Her head was spinning. That morning, she'd left for work, and spent the day knowing she had a decent boyfriend, a nice apartment, and a stable job. She came home and it seemed that two out of three of those were no longer true. She'd never understood what it meant to have her world turned upside down until Blake announced their breakup. Everything was different, and she had no control over any of it.

"I can't afford this place by myself," was all she could think to say.

Blake had been waiting on the couch when she got home, and had told her it was over. He'd consoled her for an hour, then went back to packing. Emma had spent another hour watching him walk back and forth into the living room, picking up whatever he'd missed during the day. He'd taken time off work to get a head start on removing his life from hers, one shirt at a time.

"I'll leave the furniture for the rest of the month, until you decide what you want to do. I'll have movers come get the big stuff then."

Emma snorted. How nice of him, to leave her a couch to cry on for the next three weeks while she put her life back together. He had purchased all the furniture when they moved in together. She didn't make that much money as a technical writer, and at the time, it had seemed thoughtful.

"What's mine is yours," he'd said.

There was a knock at the door, and Blake darted over to answer it.

"Billy, thanks for coming, buddy," Blake high-fived his friend, then pointed to the collection of suitcases in the center of the room.

"Just these today," he told Billy, who nodded over at Emma and had the decency not to smile.

Emma sat on the couch as Blake and Billy moved the pile of suitcases from their living room to, presumably, Billy's truck. When the room was empty, Emma heard the truck start up on the street outside, and wondered if Blake would come back up the sidewalk to say goodbye, or at the very least, close the front door.

A moment later, Emma heard his voice at the door.

"Well, I guess that's it," he said, and shrugged.

Emma shook her head.

"What happened?" she asked for the hundredth time that afternoon.

Blake sighed, but mercifully didn't check his watch again.

"It's been happening for a while, Emma. We've been growing apart. It's not you, it's us. We got stuck going through the motions, and it was time. I know this is fast, but a clean break will be easier for both of us."

Blake stepped forward, and for the first time that afternoon, touched Emma. He caressed her cheek until she looked up at him and leaned into his hand.

"We just got used to being together, but I don't think either of us was happy."

Blake pulled his hand away, then walked through the front door and closed it behind him. Emma heard his footsteps fade down the sidewalk, then the rumble of his car as it started at the curb. The engine roared as he pulled away, then the sound faded as he drove down the road. She listened for another few minutes, wondering if he would turn around. Maybe he'd forgotten something, or maybe he'd tell her he made a mistake. But the street outside stayed quiet.

"I was happy," Emma told the empty room, then sat alone on her ex-boyfriend's couch and cried.

CHAPTER 2

Emma slept on the couch that night. Every time she went into the bedroom, she saw Blake's empty drawers, still partially open, as though he couldn't pause his escape long enough to close them. The room still smelled like him. The pillow was still dented from where he'd slept next to her the night before. She lay in bed a while facing that pillow, picturing him asleep next to her, until it hurt too much and she moved to the living room, shutting the bedroom door behind her.

After a night filled with tossing and turning and a stiff neck from the couch, Emma got up and made herself a cup of coffee. Still in her pajamas, she trudged through the living room and out onto the balcony with the hot mug in her hands and sat in one of the patio chairs. They lived on the first floor in a condo complex of two-story buildings. The balcony looked onto a small path lined with grass, with identical condos mirroring theirs across the path.

It was cloudy, but Emma wore sunglasses to hide her eyes. They were aching and puffy from a night of tears and little sleep, and she didn't want any neighbors to notice. Not that they'd worry - she and Blake had lived in the condo for almost two years, and despite the close proximity to so many people, Emma didn't know any of her neighbors' names.

A door opened and slammed shut to the condo on the right, and Emma nodded a greeting to the young couple as they passed. As they walked away, Emma suppressed a small smile. Their bedroom shared a wall with Emma and Blake's, and Emma tried to recall how many times she'd woken up to passionate screams or the rhythmic banging of their headboard against the shared wall. When she and Blake moved in, Emma thought they must be newlyweds, or at least just starting out their relationship. But after nearly two years, the frequency hadn't waned, and Emma had learned to sleep with ear plugs.

She wondered, as she sipped her coffee, what they thought when she and Blake went at it, if it made them realize how thin the walls were. The thought made Emma pause.

When *was* the last time they'd had sex? Blake's birthday was in June, and she'd bought revealing lingerie for the occasion. They'd definitely had sex then, but Emma tried to think if it had happened in the months since. She remembered putting on the outfit again for a holiday weekend, but Blake had gone into the office to work, and she'd ended up switching to sweat pants and falling asleep on the couch. He was always either working or training for an upcoming marathon, and never seemed to have time for sex. Emma remembered thinking, 'once this project is over', or 'once this marathon is in the past', he'd have more time.

But maybe it wasn't the training, or the projects at work, that were keeping them apart. Maybe Blake just didn't have time for *her*.

Emma set the coffee on the small table in front of her, nauseous. How blind had she been? How long had Blake really been over the relationship, while she continued naively as though they had a future together?

She pulled her cellphone from her pocket and turned it on, then stared at the screen while it powered up. She'd turned it off in the middle of the night so that in case Blake texted or called, she wouldn't be tempted to reply immediately. Emma had wanted to make him wait, make him wonder what she was doing that kept her too busy to reply. She had wanted him to feel a fraction of how unimportant she now felt to him.

The phone finished powering on, and Emma waited. It buzzed to notify that she had new emails waiting, which all turned out to be spam, but otherwise there was nothing.

Emma sat on the balcony with her sunglasses on until past noon, watching the light move across the ledge in front of her as her phone rested silently in her lap.

CHAPTER 3

Emma spent the rest of the Saturday alternating between debilitating sadness and unrelenting fury. She broke two of Blake's favorite coffee mugs with a hammer, then spent an hour crying as she glued them back together, only to throw them in the garbage. She felt like her heart was on a rollercoaster, and all her brain could do was hang on.

Emma busied herself cleaning her apartment, trying not to look at her phone, but by dinnertime, she could see her reflection in every surface that wasn't carpeted, and Blake still hadn't called. She gave in and called his phone, wondering as it rang what she wanted to say, but she hung up when it went to voicemail. She was about to leave a voicemail that either would've been filled with crying or yelling when the phone buzzed in her hand. Emma ended the call with Blake's voicemail and checked the caller ID before answering her other line.

"Liz, hi," she answered.

"Hi Emma. Are you okay?"

"Um, yeah," she lied. "Just cleaning and hanging around the apartment. Why?"

Liz paused before clearing her throat.

"I just saw about you and Blake, and I wanted to make sure you're alright."

"What do you mean?"

"On all of his social media," Liz said. "He changed his status, and it looks like every photo of you is gone."

Emma felt her face get hot as she sat on her couch and opened her laptop. A few clicks later, she verified what Liz had told her, and that anyone who met Blake from that moment on would believe he was a single man. He'd managed to delete her existence from both his real and online lives before the weekend was over.

"Emma, are you there? I'm so sorry."

Emma sniffed, then lowered her face into her hands and sobbed.

"I'm coming over," Liz said.

"No, I'm okay, it's fine," Emma said.

"It's no trouble, really."

Emma looked back to her laptop, at Blake's smiling face looking out, alone, from the box that used to hold a picture of the two of them. She let out another sob before wiping her eyes.

"Bring wine."

Liz and Emma spent Saturday night drinking wine and updating Emma's own social media to reflect her new status, and she spent Sunday regretting the wine and the angry voicemail she'd left for Blake after Liz had left. Even with that, and her earlier phone call to Blake, he hadn't responded.

So much for wondering if he would check on her. He told her a 'clean break' would be easiest, but after three years together, she assumed he would at least call or text her after ending it to make sure she was okay.

Monday morning came around, and Emma hadn't heard anything from Blake since he said goodbye in their living room.

Correction. *Her* living room, at least for three weeks while she looked for a new place.

Emma made it to work right on time, despite spending twenty minutes crying in the bathroom after she'd found Blake's favorite cologne in the medicine cabinet. She hoped her puffy eyes looked like she was sleep-deprived rather than sad, but since she worked mainly with older males, she suspected no one would notice either way.

"Oh good, you're here."

Emma looked up from her desk to see her least favorite program manager, George Johnson, leaning against the wall of her cube. He was nearing fifty and married with two teenagers, but Emma always got the feeling that he was undressing her with his eyes.

"Good morning George, was there something you needed?"

Emma tightened her sweater around her chest as she looked up at George, wondering if he thought that his glasses hid the fact he was staring at her chest.

"Yeah, I'm going to need you to revise two sections of the manual. Our initial read-through showed we were lacking a lot of detail. We'll need more, and if you could have it done by tomorrow, that'd be great."

Before Emma could respond, George was already walking down the hallway. It was a typical interaction with him. He gave vague orders to her chest and left before she could say anything. She thought that he was intentionally vague to give himself more time to visit her cubicle, but it might've just been paranoia. Emma sighed, then swiveled her chair back to face her computer.

Seven years earlier, Emma had graduated with her masters in English from the University of San Diego. She had been determined to get a job with a magazine or newspaper, or maybe as an editor at a publishing house.

When she had trouble finding work, a friend of hers got her a job as a technical writer. The job consisted of translating technical engineer jargon into informative and legible manuals to accompany the hardware or software they were selling to the customer.

It was only temporary, Emma had always told herself, while she looked for the work she really wanted to do.

But after a few years, Emma still hadn't found her dream job, and the money was decent enough to justify sticking around while she saved up. Once a month, she put out a blog post online about her life, or her thoughts, that she'd hoped would gain a following. She was pretty sure the only visitors were Liz and her friend Marcy from college, but she enjoyed writing it, and thought eventually it might lead to something else. At the very least, it was good writing practice while she worked a job she didn't enjoy. Once she met Blake, she found happiness outside of work, and writing didn't seem as important.

Now that Blake was gone, Emma realized that she had spent seven years getting better at a job she never liked to begin with. She had no published novel, hadn't even written anything outside of the occasional blog post and her personal journal, and she was beginning to see that she'd wasted almost a decade of her life working at a small desk next to the bathrooms towards something she didn't want.

Emma rubbed her eyes, then heard her phone vibrate on her desk.

How're you holding up?

The text message was from Marcy, who had moved back to her hometown in Montana soon after graduating.

Could be better, but I'm okay, Emma texted back.

Emma had barely kept any friends from high school or college. She tried to blame it on distance or schedules, but she knew it was her own fault. Everyone seemed to be so successful and happy, getting promoted and married and pregnant, and she was in the same place she'd been since graduation. But somehow, even after seven years, she and Marcy were still friends, despite the distance.

Liar.

Emma laughed. She'd never had siblings, but she imagined that having Marcy was the next best thing. She always knew when Emma was lying, even through a text message.

You're right. I'm at my desk trying not to cry, and Jerk George just came by and ogled me, Emma wrote.

I keep telling you to report him, Marcy wrote back.

I know, but he never does anything specific enough to report. Just the occasional stare and overall condescension, like the rest of this place, Emma wrote.

She was in an especially negative mood, but she wasn't exaggerating too much. Her office was filled with intelligent men with huge egos and to many of them she was a secretary from the 1950s.

A reminder popped up on Emma's computer, and she texted Marcy again.

Thanks for checking in, she wrote. *I have a meeting in five minutes, but I'll talk to you later.*

Call me after work! I want to talk to you about something, Marcy replied.

Will do.

Emma dropped her phone into her desk drawer, then grabbed a notebook and pen and headed down the hall to the conference room for her meeting.

"Now, these geometry and bolt modifications will require that we update the documentation. There won't be any functional changes, but we still need to make sure we capture it in any images. Emma, does that make sense?"

Emma nodded, biting her tongue. She may not have gotten an engineering degree, but she'd been working around engineers for years, and understood more about machining processes and fastener types than she had ever cared to. In addition, George had already sent out an email listing the required updates, and Emma had contacted the responsible engineer for images the week before and put them into the manual. If she thought it would shorten the meeting, Emma would have mentioned that the work was already done, but she'd learned years earlier that her managers seemed to view meetings as evidence of their own productivity.

"Great," George continued. "We're hoping to get a first draft by the end of this week. Do you think that's reasonable?"

"That's fine," she answered, mentally willing George to move on.

The meeting had already lasted over an hour, with the first twenty minutes spent discussing how long of an extension cord they should buy for the projector in the new conference room. Emma didn't want to be at work or around people, pretending that her life hadn't fallen apart over the weekend. She didn't have any friends at the office, and no one wanted the real answer to 'how was your weekend?'. So until she left for the day and went back to her apartment, alone, Emma was faking happiness while fighting back tears. It was exhausting.

After another ten minutes, the meeting ended, and Emma went back to her cubicle. She waited an hour before sending the updated documentation to George for review, then spent the rest of the afternoon answering emails and trying not to think about Blake. By the time she got in her car to drive home, all she wanted was to put her pajamas back on and lay on the couch in the dark.

She unlocked her apartment door and walked inside, forgetting for a moment that Blake wouldn't be there. He worked closer to the apartment than she did, which was the main reason they lived there. He usually beat her home by half an hour, and was either watching sports or sitting on the couch with his laptop when Emma got home.

But today, the apartment was quiet except for hum of the ceiling fan she'd left on in the living room.

Emma sighed and dropped her purse by the door before shutting and locking it behind her. She went into the bedroom and changed into her pajamas, then closed it behind her and pulled a bottle of white wine from the refrigerator. As she was pouring herself a glass, her cell phone rang from her purse. She trotted to the door, realizing as her heart sped that she hoped it was Blake.

"Hi Marcy," she said after checking the caller ID.

"Hi!" Marcy always sounded cheerful, regardless of what was going on in her life. "I know I told you to call me, but I couldn't wait. How are you?"

Emma walked back to the kitchen to get her wine glass and leaned against the counter as she drank.

"I don't know. Numb, I think," she said.

"Have you heard from Blake?"

"Nope. I guess he meant it when he said he wanted a clean break."

"I'm sorry," Marcy answered.

"No you aren't," Emma countered.

Marcy had only met Blake once during a visit from Montana, but she hadn't been able to hide her dislike for him whenever Emma brought him up in conversation.

"Just because I didn't like the guy doesn't mean I'm not sorry you're hurting," Marcy answered.

"You just didn't get to know him."

"I know I only met him that one time, but he just seemed so... shallow. All he talked about when I was there was his marathon training and how fast he was. And all I ever heard from you was how he put you down about your exercise. He didn't even read your blog."

"I was just venting when I talked to you. I didn't need to vent about all the good things," Emma answered, but part of her knew Marcy had a point.

Once Blake had started training for the marathon, he had made more and more comments about how Emma would look and feel so much better if she exercised, how she should eat better. And it was true that he had never been very supportive of her blog. She wasn't sure the last time he'd even read it. Somehow her dream to be a writer was less noble than his dream to run long distances.

"Emma, *were* there any good things?" Marcy asked, and Emma sighed.

"I don't know anymore," she answered, and took a long sip of wine.

They sat on the phone in silence for a minute before Marcy spoke.

"Well, I am sorry that you're hurting. I'll just say that I think you're smart and beautiful and wonderful, and there is someone out there who will see all of those qualities and raise you up rather than put you down."

"Thanks," Emma whispered, and swiped her hand against the tears welling up in her eyes.

"Now, the second reason I called," Marcy said, sounding even more excited than usual. "Do you still have copies of any of the stories you wrote in college for the newspaper?"

Emma blinked at the subject change.

"That's a little out of left field. Why do you ask?"

"My niece is joining her high school newspaper, and I thought she could use some examples."

"I'm sure you have newspapers up in Montana that she could study from," Emma answered.

"Yeah, but that's all local news and world news. I think that the college level would be more relevant to what she'd be working on," Marcy explained. "Plus you did all those great features on athletes, professors, students – she wants to do features too, and your writing was so fantastic, I just thought yours would be a better example for her."

Emma raised her eyebrows, wondering what Marcy was really up to. She talked faster when she lied, and she spat out her last sentence so quickly that Emma could barely understand her.

"I think I have them somewhere," she started, refilling her wine glass before heading towards the patio. "But I think your memory is foggy. They weren't that great, just basic profiles."

Emma had been proud of the articles at the time, had even hung a few on her wall when she lived alone. She had shown them to Blake when they first started dating, and he'd complimented her, but somehow they never made it back onto the wall after they moved in together.

"Your brain is the foggy one," Marcy answered.

"I don't know," Emma said, as she pulled open the sliding glass door to the patio. "Son of a bitch!"

"What? Are you okay?" Marcy asked.

Emma shook her head and could almost feel the steam coming out of her ears.

"He took the damn patio furniture," Emma said.

In front of her, where there once was a full patio set and potted plant, was now an empty cement floor with a few scattered leaves where the plant used to sit.

"I thought he wasn't taking anything until the end of the lease?" Marcy asked.

Emma snorted.

"Apparently he changed his mind. I was here all weekend, so he must've come in today while I was at work."

The man couldn't call or text to check on her, but snuck into the apartment when he knew she would be gone to take whatever he wanted.

"What a jerk," Marcy said, and Emma nodded.

She had spent most of her hangover the day before on that patio, watching the sky turn from light to grey to black, then light again. Watching the sun brighten the dark, endless night, had been the first glimpse Emma had that there might be hope. The sun could rise every day, regardless of what terrible things happened, and maybe so could she.

And Blake had come and taken the chair away that had been the spot for that realization. Somehow the theft felt like he had damaged hope itself, and seemed almost worse than breaking up with her in the first place.

"Emma? Are you okay?" Marcy asked.

"I'm fine," she said through clenched teeth. "I'll send you the articles tonight," she said, and Marcy cheered.

"Thank you!"

"No problem. I'll talk to you later," Emma said, hanging up the phone. She'd deleted Blake's number from her phone, but still had it memorized, and opened a new text message. She thought for a minute, staring at the empty white box, before typing.

Thief.

Emma sent the message and drained the rest of her glass of wine before refilling it, then grabbed her laptop and sat on the couch. All of her work from college would be on external hard drives, which were in a box in the back of the closet. She would get to those, but there was something more important she needed to do first.

Emma took a sip of wine, then opened her internet browser and typed in 'patio furniture'.

"I hated that old set, anyway," she mumbled to herself, then let her anger fill the spaces that for the past three days, only sadness had occupied.

CHAPTER 4

Emma spent the next few days trying to keep her sadness at bay and hold onto the anger for Blake, who still hadn't called or responded to her voicemail or texts, but thankfully hadn't taken anything else from the apartment. Nothing that she noticed, anyway.

At work, she managed to keep her anger in check, which proved difficult with a boss like George. He sent her multiple revision comments, some of which contradicted themselves, and Emma had to keep herself from replying to his emails with, 'Just figure out what you want and make a decision, already.'

She wondered how it would have turned out with Blake if she'd said something similar to him when their sex life had dwindled, when he had more time for work and running than he did for her. If she'd sat next to him while he worked at his laptop on the couch and made him look at her, listen to her. What if she'd noticed that the 'rough patch' was really just Blake leaving the relationship without her, while she still had held out hope that things would get better?

Would she be over him already, or would they still have had a chance to be together?

As Emma checked her phone for the thousandth time in six days and found that she hadn't gotten so much as an email from Blake, she knew the answer was no.

How could she have been so blind?

Emma jumped as the phone buzzed in her hand, and she answered in a whisper, "Hi Marcy, give me a second."

Emma hated talking on the phone in her cubicle. The office was so quiet that she could hear the person in the cubicle adjacent to hers chewing during lunch, so she knew anything she said would be subject to eavesdropping. She walked to the nearest exit and wandered into the parking lot.

"Okay, sorry, I had to walk outside. What's up?"

"Oh nothing," Marcy said, but Emma could hear the smile in her voice. "Just checking in to see how you're doing."

"Well, I'm at work, so things could be better," she answered. "I decided to wait on the new patio furniture until I get a new place and figure out what will fit."

"That's probably a good plan," Marcy said. "Speaking of a new place, I had a thought."

"Did you?" Emma asked.

"Do you remember my grandparents? I think you met them one summer a few years ago when you came to visit."

Emma thought for a second.

"When I came for Fourth of July? I think I remember that. Their neighbors lit off fireworks, and we had a barbeque at your grandparents' cabin."

"That's it!" Marcy exclaimed.

"What's it?"

"The cabin," Marcy answered.

"What about the cabin?"

"That can be your new place!"

Emma took in a deep breath, then let it out at once, shaking her head.

"Marcy, you've lost me," Emma said, leaning against a tree at the edge of the parking lot next to the sidewalk. She picked at the bark on the tree, pulling off small chunks and tossing them to the ground.

"My grandparents don't like spending winter in Montana anymore, and they've been leaving earlier and earlier every year. This year, they're leaving in a week and driving their RV to Seattle to visit my aunt for a month before they head south."

Marcy paused, but Emma waited to find out why the travel plans of an elderly couple she'd met once five years earlier would matter to her.

"They're renting out their cabin while they're gone, and I told them you were interested! Since you're one of my best friends, they'll give you a really good deal."

"But I live here," was all Emma could think to say.

"Right, but you need to move out in a couple of weeks. By then, my grandparents will be gone and the cabin could be all yours. It's furnished and everything, so you'd just need to bring your clothes and personal things."

"That's sweet of you to offer, Marcy, but-"

"But what?" Marcy interrupted. "Your relationship with the guy who made you feel bad about yourself is over and your lease is almost up. It's the perfect time for a change."

Emma's head was spinning. Marcy was sweet to try to help her, but this much change felt like a bit of an overcorrection.

"You're not wrong," Emma said. "But moving to Montana? I loved the area, and the quiet, but to move there seems a little drastic. Plus, I can't move without a job. I have some money saved, but not enough to live without a job indefinitely."

"That's the best part!" Marcy shouted, and Emma had to pull the phone away from her ear. "I got you a job!"

"What?"

"Well technically it's a job and a part-time internship. My mom's friend has an uncle who runs a magazine in town. The magazine runs an internship program, and I applied for you. I used your old articles and your blog, and I think you're in! You just have to set up a time to do a phone interview, which I'm sure will be no big deal."

Emma opened her mouth, but nothing came out. She had guessed Marcy was up to something when she'd asked for Emma's writing samples, but she thought Marcy was just going to frame them or put them in a scrapbook as a gift. Using them to get Emma an internship was not something she would have guessed.

"Emma? Did you hear me?"

"I did," Emma stammered. "But I'm confused. How can I do an internship? I'm not in college."

"It isn't strictly for college students, that's just usually who applies. We made sure with Don, and he said he gives opportunities to any good writers with excellent work ethic, which I assured him you have. Anyway, a few of the previous interns have moved onto being full-time employees. If it worked out, you could be a full-time writer at a magazine."

The young college girl who still lived somewhere inside Emma's mind jumped up and down. It had been her dream all through college to work at a magazine or newspaper. Her job as a technical writer was only supposed to be temporary, but eventually she had forgotten she once had passion for a different dream. But it turned out there was still an ember lingering from that old fire, a desire for a dream that she'd all but forgotten about.

"I don't know, Marcy. The internship sounds great, but I'd still need a job."

"That's the second exciting news," Marcy said. "My brother just opened a second location for his coffee shop, and he needs to hire at least two full-time employees for the original location. It won't quite pay what you're making down there, but since the rent is way cheaper at the cabin, I think it should be enough."

"Marcy, I haven't worked at a coffee shop since college."

"I know, but it's just like riding a bike. You were assistant manager by the time we graduated, so I know you know how to do it. It isn't technical papers, but the schedule is flexible, so you could work around the internship. And we'd get to see each other all the time!"

Emma took another deep breath and looked up at the bright blue San Diego sky.

"Look Emma, I know this is a lot at once. But what have you got to lose?" Marcy asked.

Before Emma could answer, Marcy jumped in.

"Shoot, my lunch break is over. At least just talk to Don. He's supposed to email you to set up a time."

"Okay," Emma said. "Bye Marcy."

Emma hung up the phone, but stayed against the tree. She knew she would say no. How could she just quit her job and move out of state to work at a coffee shop? Wouldn't that be a step in the wrong direction? And an internship she wasn't even close to qualified for? Maybe it was a dream she wanted once, but maybe it wasn't what she thought it would be. Maybe she'd be terrible.

Her phone buzzed in her hand, and she opened it to find an email from Don, requesting to set up a time later that day to talk.

Despite her fears, she could feel the ember inside her catch a spark. She agreed to Don's proposed time and sent the email before she could back out, then walked back to her office. She spent the next few hours alternating between scanning articles in Don's magazine and staring at the clock on her computer screen, wondering if being terrible at something she wanted could be worse than being good at something she didn't.

At two minutes before five o'clock, Emma sat on her living room couch, staring at her cellphone on the coffee table in front of her. She'd left work early so that she could be home in time to take Don's call. She hadn't been on an interview in years, and the sound of her heartbeat pounding in her ears and the warmth of her face reminded her how nervous they'd always made her.

The phone buzzed on the table in front of her, and Emma saw an unfamiliar number flash across the screen.

"Hello, this is Emma," she said, then took a deep breath after hearing the tremble in her voice.

"Emma, thanks for taking the time. This is Don from the Missoula Reader. How are you this evening?"

"I'm great, Don, thanks for calling me. How are you?"

"The sun is shining and my wife is making pot roast for dinner, so I can't complain."

"That's good to hear," Emma said, picking at a loose thread in the couch cushion next to her.

"Well, let's get to it," he said, and Emma took another deep breath. "Marcy sent over some old college articles of yours, and I've read your blog. Normally we don't have applications submitted by people other than the applicant, but Marcy is incredibly difficult to ignore."

"That she is," Emma answered, nodding.

"She might've also told you that we usually fill these internships with local college students, but that isn't a requirement. We've made exceptions in the past, so don't think I'm just talking to you as a favor to a friend. Like I said, I enjoyed your blog."

"Thank you," Emma said. Her heart was still pounding away behind her ribcage, but the compliment helped her to keep breathing.

"I will say that I see potential there, but I think there are areas in your writing that you may need guidance on, which is why I think Marcy feels you'd be a good fit for this internship. I'd tend to agree, but I do have a few questions for you before we go any further."

"Of course," Emma said.

"Now first, why don't you explain to me what you do currently? I understand it is writing, but not exactly what we do here."

"That's correct," Emma replied, straightening her back. "I'm a technical writer, so I mainly work with engineers to create manuals or documentation for their products, either for internal use or for our customers."

"Got it. What do you like about it?"

Emma fought against her gut response, which was to say 'it pays the bills', and took another breath.

"I like learning new things. I went to college for journalism, so learning about different bolt installation methods wasn't something I thought I would encounter. Even if it wasn't something I envisioned myself doing, I think it has been useful. I think I've developed an attention to detail and ability to research new subjects that I don't think I'd explored in depth during college."

There was a pause on the other end of the line, and Emma was about to check her phone to make sure the call didn't drop when she heard the flip of a piece of paper, and assumed Don was taking notes.

"And why do you think you want to take an internship at the magazine?"

Emma bit her lip. Why did she want to leave her job to go back to working at a coffee shop? Why did she want to leave her now-empty apartment and life in San Diego?

"Well, as you've seen, I have my blog, so I've been telling my story. But I think that everyone deserves a time in the spotlight. Everyone should have a chance to tell their own story. From reading your magazine, I think that's what you do best. Even in a story about a high school basketball game, it's really about the kids playing, their backgrounds, and their dreams. I want to be a part of that."

"Hmm," Don said, and Emma waited for Don's next question. "Well Emma, I think that's all I have for you. You were the last interview of the day, so I'll be reviewing everything with our HR supervisor. We should be getting in touch either way within the next few days."

"Sounds good, Don. Thank you for taking the time to talk to me."

"Thank you, Emma," Don answered.

Emma hung up her phone and set it on her coffee table before taking another huge breath.

She felt like she'd done well, but she didn't want to get too hopeful. Even if it was just an internship, it was more in line with what she'd always wanted to do, and she was afraid to be too confident. She was competing against college students who likely lived in Montana, and she was a nearly-thirty recently-dumped technical writer with a blog no one read.

Emma paced back and forth in the living room a handful of times before going into the closet in her bedroom to pull a box from the corner. Inside were at least five journals dating from when she first learned to write when she was a child up through college. She had a small notebook where she kept funny or motivating quotes she'd heard or read, and another notebook filled with the lovesick poetry she was obsessed with writing when she was in high school.

She perused the contents, her crushes in middle school and her frustrations through high school, before laying them back into the box. She walked to her bedside table and pulled a small blue book from the drawer and sat on the edge of her bed. Emma pulled it out and flipped to the first page, where there was a sticky note.

For all of your post-college experiences. Keep on writing! - Marcy

It had been Emma's graduation gift from college. She'd filled two journals during college, and Marcy always commented that the pages would eventually turn into Emma's first memoir. The gift was meant to mark Emma's transition into 'the real world'. She flipped through the pages, reading every few entries. They started hopeful, but each failed interview made the entries space farther and farther apart. Emma read the entry from when she got the job as a technical writer, promising herself in writing that she'd look for something better once she had built her savings and gotten more experience.

But she hadn't looked. She didn't know if it was the fear of more rejection or the comfort in knowing what was going to happen every day, but once Emma sat in her chair at work, it was like she didn't see a reason to get back up.

Emma flipped through the pages, noting that the entries picked up in frequency when she had met Blake, then dwindled again over the past year. Her last entry was months earlier, and she'd written about Blake's upcoming marathon and the fact that she hoped she got a bonus at Christmas so that she could accompany him to the race in Boston the following year.

Emma shook her head, turning over the next few blank pages before taking the journal into the closet and sliding it inside the box alongside all her other journals. She grabbed her coat and purse, then left the apartment.

Back at home, Emma sat on her balcony, looking up at the sky as it darkened. She'd laid a towel down the night before to keep her clothes from getting too dirty, and she sat down on it and set her wine glass beside her. It was late summer and the sun was still out, so she didn't need the patio light on just yet.

She took a sip of wine from her glass and set it down next to her, then looked down, where a brand new journal sat on her lap. The liquor store across the street had limited options, so she went with a green one with gold-rimmed pages. She opened the book to the first page, bright white and empty, and held her pen up to it. She wrote the date in the corner and moved her hand down, then froze.

What did she have to say?

The last page in Emma's college journal was written by a young woman who was standing at the beginning of her future, full of hope and optimism and a desire for a big, exciting life. The last page of her existing journal was of a woman who seemed to be marking time, who had given up on herself.

And who was the girl at the first page of this empty notebook? What had happened in the years between those last two books that had led Emma to this spot on the ground, alone and unhappy? Where had her dreams gone, and why had she let them go? Who had she become? Who could she still become? Her talk with Don seemed to have gone well, but would she take the internship if he offered it? And if he didn't offer it, what would she do? Would she just go back to her life and forget what hope felt like?

After ten minutes of questioning everything that had brought her to this moment in her life, Emma put her pen to the first page of the empty book and wrote two words.

What now?

CHAPTER 5

Emma brought her notebook to work with her the next morning. She hadn't written anything else the night before, but she thought carrying it around with her would help keep the thought of writing in it at the front of her mind. She set it on her desk when she got to work, and kept it in her line of sight as she checked her emails.

George had sent her an email late the night before, asking her to revise her latest manual back to the way she had it the week before. Since she'd gotten used to his ever-changing needs, Emma never wrote over any copies of her work, but rather saved revisions with notes of what she had changed with each update. As she was going through folders to find the version that reflected George's latest desires, her phone buzzed on her desk.

Emma picked up her phone and felt her heart pounding in her chest as she saw that the email came from Don. She took a deep breath before opening the email, telling herself that whatever happened, it didn't matter. But when she realized that she was holding her breath, she knew she was lying to herself. A door had opened inside of her, and it wasn't going to be closed easily. When she finished reading the email, she let out a breath and smiled.

She'd been offered the internship.

Before she could take another full breath, a knock came on her cubicle wall.

She swiveled around to see George at her cubicle, along with her boss, Brandon Hughes. Brandon was in his late sixties and, while he was less blatant about his physical ogling, Emma got the feeling he talked more slowly to her than the male employees, as though she needed more explanation than everyone else.

"Are you free for a chat, Ms. Ward?" Mr. Hughes glanced at Emma's phone, then back to her, and smiled.

She could hear two of her coworkers in the aisle over talking about the baseball game from the night before with excruciating detail, but somehow checking her phone was cause for admonishment. The double standard was palpable.

"Yes, I'm free. What can I do for you?" Emma set the phone back down on her desk, but the words in the email kept flashing through her mind.

Brandon folded his arms.

"Well, George here says he asked you to update a few sections of that manual for the San Francisco customer."

"He did," Emma answered, trying to fight the smile from growing too big on her face. "I was just digging out the version that has the images you asked for in your email," Emma answered. "Was there something else that needed updating?" she asked, looking from George to her boss and back.

"Well, George was afraid you might not have understood what he wanted, so we thought we should come clarify for you." Mr. Hughes folded his hands in front of him and smiled down at her as though she were a dog who couldn't quite figure out how to sit.

"No, I think I get it. I'd already sent him a version that reflects what he asked for last week, but changed it based on the meeting Monday. I have the original version on my computer. I can email it to you both, if you'd like."

Then they could also leave her office, Emma thought, and George would have to stop staring at her chest as though he was waiting for his X-Ray vision to activate so he could see through her sweater.

"Well, you could email it, but after all this back and forth, I figured it would be easier if we all just sat down and went through it together," George said, managing to pull his eyes from her cleavage while he spoke this time. She was surprised he didn't pull a muscle in his neck from the strain.

That's it, Emma thought. Corroboration or not, HR was going to get an earful.

"Yes, we want to make sure you don't miss anything important," Mr. Hughes said, still smiling at her like she was a grandchild rather than a coworker.

"Well, if the changes are what George told me to implement last week, I have the version right here. I only modified the file based on what George asked for Monday," she said again.

Were they always so patronizing, or was she only noticing today because she had nothing else to distract her? Blake was gone, she had another job opportunity, and she suddenly realized that all of the men in her life had been treating her like shit?

"I think face to face would probably work better, if you can find the time?" Mr. Hughes asked.

We'd like to offer you an internship, Emma replayed in her head.

Emma glanced at her phone, then looked back up at her boss, who was still smiling at her in a way that made her want to scream. Then she looked over at George, whose gaze had moved from her eyes back to her chest, as though a tractor beam connected the two.

Emma looked at the nearly empty journal on her desk and ran her fingertip down the binding. What would the pages inside reveal if she stayed here? Would they stay blank, and would she eventually drop the book back into a box in the back of her closet? Would the dreams of her youth be officially lost and forgotten, buried in the dark as she trudged along in a safe but unfulfilling future?

What would those blank pages look like if she didn't stay?

"So, Emma, do you have the time for us?" Mr. Hughes asked, then took a step forward to one of the guest chairs against the wall inside her cubicle.

"No," she said, and Brandon stopped smiling. "I quit."

CHAPTER 6

Two weeks later, Emma found herself driving north on Interstate 15 in her sixteen-year-old Honda, wishing she'd taken the time to get the air conditioning fixed before she left. It was the end of August, so the peak of the summer heat had passed, but it was still too warm to drive with the windows up.

She stopped for lunch when she hit Las Vegas, wondering for the millionth time what the hell she was doing. After telling her boss that she was quitting, Emma had spent the rest of the day cleaning out her desk, talking to HR, and wondering if she'd just made the biggest mistake of her life.

She'd spent the following two weeks packing everything she could fit in her small car, and selling off what was left. She had debated either selling or donating the furniture Blake had said he would pick up, but in the end had decided on neither. While her anger was still as bright as a hot poker in a flame, she thought that doing anything with his property would only mean she'd have to talk to him. Or talk *at* him, since he still hadn't returned her calls. She had called him one last time to let him know that she had vacated the apartment, but didn't say anything else in her voicemail.

The only person who seemed to really care that Emma was leaving was Liz. Aside from coming over when Emma and Blake broke up, Liz and Emma usually met up once a month for their B.I.G. nights – booze, ice cream, and gossip. Liz had been Emma's friend for nearly a decade, and seemed to be the only one who would actually miss her. The thought made her wonder, not for the first time, how much of the last few years was worth anything.

Emma got back out on the road after lunch and drove through empty desert for hours, watching the sky change colors in the rearview mirror as the sun set on the horizon. As soon as she crossed the Utah border, the only radio stations she could find without static played country music, so she shut it off and listened to the wind push against her ears.

At nearly ten o'clock, Emma drove into Salt Lake City, and pulled off the freeway as soon as she saw a hotel sign. She was too tired to keep going for much longer, and she wasn't sure how limited the hotel options would be north of a big city like Salt Lake.

Emma locked her car and walked from the warm September night into the cool hotel lobby. A young blonde behind the desk smiled as Emma approached, her teeth gleaming under the bright hotel lights.

"Well hi there, welcome," she said.

Emma looked around for the empty gallon of coffee the girl must have stored nearby, but saw nothing. Either she was hiding it under the desk, or she really was that upbeat this late at night.

"Hi, thanks," Emma said, trying to match the girl's tone but failing miserably after half a day in a hot car. "I was wondering if I could get a room for the night?"

The vacancy sign out front was lit, so Emma assumed there would be room for her.

"Absolutely. How long will you need it for?"

"Just the night, thanks."

"Great, wonderful," the girl said, and began typing away at her computer.

Emma noticed her name tag said Brooke, and realized she had never met a Brooke who wasn't blonde and cheerful. Maybe it was a requirement that came with the name. Or all of the Brookes grew into it, the way a goldfish's size was determined by the bowl it lived in.

"How many beds will you need?" Brooke asked, glancing through the lobby towards the entrance.

"Just me, so just the one bed, thanks," Emma said.

Brooke tapped away at her computer a bit more, then gave Emma the price and amenities information while she made Emma's room keys.

"Where are you coming from?"

"San Diego," Emma answered.

"Oh, San Diego. My husband and I just love it there," Brooke said, smiling even wider as she handed Emma the keys to her room.

Husband, Emma thought. Something about the word cut into Emma's heart. Here she was, nearly thirty and traveling alone, while this girl who was barely spitting distance from twenty was already married and going traveling with her husband. Emma must look ancient to her.

"Have a great night, and let us know if you need anything!"

Emma smiled and picked up her bag, then walked herself to the elevator. Blake was training for a marathon, so she had been trying to get in better shape over the past few months and had forced herself to take the stairs whenever possible.

But she had just been dumped, quit her job, driven nearly eight hundred miles, and finally been made to feel an old spinster by a girl who probably still fit into her high school cheer uniform.

Tonight was an elevator night.

Emma got to her room and threw her small travel bag, purse, and a box on the bed. She'd left most of her things in the car and parked near the hotel entrance in the hopes no one would be tempted to steal anything, even though there wasn't much worth taking. The only real valuables she had were her laptop, which she had in her bag, and what she carried in the small box on the bed.

Emma quickly changed into pajamas and brushed her teeth, then sat on the bed and opened the box of journals. It seemed strange that for the better part of a decade, Emma hadn't given a second thought to that box, and suddenly it was all she could think about.

She pulled out the journal that lay on top of the stack, the new book that she bought to represent the change she was making.

Emma turned to the first page, to her tentatively written 'What now?' and stared at it for a minute before flipping to the next empty page. She wrote the date in the corner, then held her pen against the first line.

What now? She wrote again.

She tapped her pen against the page as she looked out the window at the dark Utah night. Emma had never been to Utah before, and had checked into the hotel after the sun had already gone down, so she could only imagine what it looked

like outside her window.   She looked back at the open
notebook on her lap.

Now I try to remember what hope looks like.

CHAPTER 7

Emma got up early the following morning and took advantage of the hotel's free breakfast. The coffee wasn't the best she'd ever had, but it was hot and free, which made it taste that much better. She had a bagel and cream cheese with a side of eggs, and told herself that she would start her diet back up as soon as she got settled in Montana. She did admit to herself that she had enjoyed eating a heaping pile of good food without being judged by the health-obsessed Blake.

Thankfully, none of the hotel staff stopped by her table to be cheerful while Emma was still trying to wake up, and she was on the road by seven-thirty. Without any long stops, Emma figured she would be in Missoula by late that afternoon. She sent Marcy a quick text message as soon as she got in her car, partly to let her know when to expect her, and partly to keep herself from turning back around. Marcy responded almost immediately, and Emma got back onto the freeway headed north.

Salt Lake City was the last large town on Emma's route, and it was a Friday, so she hit a little traffic as she left the city, but the rest of her drive was uneventful. She only stopped three times - twice for gas and once to grab a burger from a drive-through, so she began seeing signs for Missoula just before four o'clock.

She pulled over to double check the address Marcy had given her, and soon after found herself pulling into a small dirt driveway lined with tall pine trees. Fifty yards down the dirt, Emma pulled up to a small one-story log cabin beside a car that must be Marcy's truck, and turned off her engine.

Emma got out of her car and shut the door behind her, then looked around. There were just three small houses that she could see from the driveway - one across the road, and two others that sat at least half a mile from where she stood on either side of the property. Otherwise, it was just trees and dirt all around her.

"You're here!" Marcy's voice carried through the quiet, and Emma looked up to see her friend bounding off the small porch onto the wild grass in front of the house.

Emma smiled as Marcy ran up and hugged her. Tight as it was, the hug squeezed out any lingering doubts Emma had about her decision. Nobody was as sad to see Emma leave as Marcy was glad to have her. And that was worth something.

"I'm here," Emma said, aiming for excited but landing somewhere closer to trepidation.

"Don't worry, you'll love it here," Marcy said, reading Emma's emotions as though they hadn't missed any time together.

"Let me show you around," Marcy said, linking her arm through Emma's as she led her towards the porch.

"My grandparents' land is five acres, so it extends to the creek on the south and west sides, and the road borders it on the north side. The Beckmans have a fence on their side, so that's as far as it goes to the east."

Emma looked around as Marcy spoke, speechless. Her townhouse with Blake shared walls on both sides, and the small balcony had barely enough room for their patio furniture. Through the trees, Emma thought she could make out the dip in the property that looked to be where the creek ran through. She would have to take a walk later to get a better idea, but from here, she realized how glad she was that she had waited to buy new patio furniture. She could fit more than just a couple chairs on this property.

"And here's the house. I'm not sure how much time we spent inside when you were here, so let me give you the grand tour," Marcy said, pushing open the large wooden door in front of them. The door itself was split in two halves, a top and bottom, so Emma could lock the bottom and leave the top open if she wanted to let air in.

The door opened into a small kitchen with a round wooden table in the right corner, while the appliances and counter lined the left side of the kitchen. Flowered drapes hung from the windows that let in light from both sides of the room. Emma hadn't been inside a log cabin since she visited Marcy in college, but it was just as cozy as she remembered.

"My grandpa built the cabin back in the sixties, before they knew they'd have eight kids. They kept it in the family when they moved into town, so all of us have had a turn living here," Marcy explained as she led Emma from the kitchen into the living room. Similar flowery curtains hung in this room as in the kitchen, and an overstuffed sofa and loveseat sat around a large rock fireplace.

"Holy cow, that fireplace is enormous," Emma said, and Marcy laughed.

"That was Grandma's doing," Marcy explained. "Grandpa originally built a smaller one, but after their first winter here together, Grandma said she'd divorce him if she ever had to be that cold again. This thing will heat the entire house all winter if you keep your woodpile stocked."

Marcy glanced at Emma's dubious expression and laughed again.

"Don't worry, my brothers clear away the dead trees for my grandparents to make sure they always have wood, so there's a giant pile outside by the shed under a few tarps. You have enough for at least two winters with what's out there."

"Fantastic," Emma said, realizing she couldn't remember the last time she'd built a fire. She hadn't had a fireplace in any apartment she had rented in San Diego, and almost never used a heater.

"Moving on," Marcy said, pointing to the left, "the bathroom is just through that door there. And up here is the bedroom."

Marcy led Emma past the fireplace to a room just on the other side, where she discovered that the fireplace had another window into the bedroom.

"Trust me, you will never get cold in here if you get that fire going really well."

Emma nodded as she stared at the queen-sized bed covered in a colorful plaid quilt and lots of pillows, realizing how tired she was. After a long three weeks, she had finally arrived at her new home, and her brain was starting to relax.

"One more thing on the tour, then I'll leave you alone for a while," Marcy said, again reading Emma's mind.

"I'm okay," Emma said, stifling a yawn.

"So just through this door is another little porch," Marcy said, pulling open the sliding glass door on the wall opposite the fireplace. Two rocking chairs sat on a small wooden porch just outside the bedroom, and a small planter box was on the ground just beyond it.

"Do your grandparents garden?" Emma asked. She had always wanted to try gardening, but never had the room. Space was definitely not a factor at the cabin.

"Grandma used to," Marcy said, nodding. "Although there was once a fence around this part back here so the deer couldn't get to it. They'll eat anything. The fence rotted a few years ago, so we pulled it out. My grandparents aren't really here during the spring anymore anyway, which was when she used to plant. Do you have a green thumb?"

Emma shrugged.

"I don't know, really."

"Well, if you're still here in the spring, maybe you could start something. I know Grandma would love to come home to it. But you'd have to do something about the deer, I'm telling you. They even ate the jalapenos she planted one year."

"Wow," Emma said, yawning again.

"Okay okay, I can take a hint," Marcy said. "How about I help you unload your car, then you take a nap?"

As little as Emma wanted to unload her car at that moment, she knew she would much rather do it with help than without.

In just under an hour, they had Emma's bags and boxes piled in a corner of the living room floor, and Emma was waving at Marcy from her front porch as she pulled down the dirt driveway and onto the street. Emma promised Marcy that she would call as soon as she was done napping so they could meet for dinner or drinks, but Marcy just laughed.

"I'll talk to you tomorrow," she kept saying, despite Emma's claim that she just needed to lay down for a few minutes.

Emma took one last look in her car, then trudged up the steps into her new home and locked the door behind her. She kicked off her flip-flops in the living room and exchanged her jeans for a pair of flannel pajama pants before climbing into her new bed.

"Just a few hours," she told herself, yawning again as she snuggled down into a bed she could swear was made purely from a cloud. She tucked the quilt around her face and closed her eyes, feeling, for the second time that day, that she had made the right decision.

"Just a few hours," she muttered again, then fell asleep.

CHAPTER 8

Emma woke to sunlight on her face, and a light tapping at her front door. She blinked a few times before opening her eyes completely, and it took almost a full minute for her brain to catch up with what she saw around her.

"Log cabin. Montana," she said, then heard the tapping at her door again.

Emma sat up, all of her muscles aching with protest. She grabbed the clock on the table beside the bed and saw that it was after eight o'clock. She wasn't used to it being light so late, but she was a few thousand miles north of San Diego, so she knew the sun set later than she was used to.

She heard a muffled, "Yoohoo," coming from the front of the house, so Emma swung her legs out of bed and shuffled to the door, combing her hair with her fingers as she went.

She moved the wooden latch across the door to unlock it, then grabbed the large wooden handle and pulled the heavy door open. Just on the other side of the door, standing on her front porch, was a tiny woman with big red hair holding a foil-covered dish and smiling.

"Hi," Emma said, blinking against the blinding sunlight, and the woman smiled wider. The wrinkles in her face as she smiled indicated she was at least in her eighties, but her hair was a brighter red than any Emma had ever seen, with lipstick to match.

"Well hi to you too, dear," the woman said, still smiling. "You must be Emma. I'm Maxine. I live just across the street there," she said, gesturing with her head to the house across the road.

"Hi Maxine," Emma said, still waking up and confused as to how the woman already knew who she was.

"Mind if I set this down on your table there? My arms aren't what they used to be," Maxine said, glancing down at the dish in her arms.

"Oh, of course, I'm so sorry. Come on in," Emma said, and stepped aside to let Maxine into the kitchen.

"Gloria told me she'd be renting this out to a friend of her granddaughter's," Maxine said, looking around the kitchen before setting her dish on the counter. "I thought about stopping by yesterday, but I figured you might still be getting settled in."

"Oh, I only got in earlier today," Emma said, following Maxine as she journeyed into the living room.

Maxine turned back and looked at Emma as though she'd grown horns.

"No, I saw you pull in yesterday, about four o'clock. I can see your front door from my porch."

Emma shook her head slightly to clear the cobwebs from her brain, immediately regretting it as she felt a sharp tug in the muscles of her neck.

"What time is it?" she asked, realizing that the clock in her bedroom must be broken.

"Eight o'clock Saturday morning," Maxine said.

"Holy crap!" Emma shouted, then apologized when Maxine raised her eyebrows. "Sorry, I just didn't realize I'd slept through the night. I must've been more exhausted than I thought."

"Change will do that to you," Maxine said, nodding.

Emma rubbed a sore spot on her back, thankful to understand that her body was stiff because she hadn't moved for fifteen hours, rather than because her body had also decided to give up on her in her time of need.

"Yes, the cabin is definitely much different than my apartment in San Diego," Emma agreed, her shoulders cracking as she rolled and loosened them.

"And the internship, and the boyfriend," Maxine rattled off, and Emma turned to look at her.

"I've visited Marcy and her grandma as they got the place ready for you," Maxine explained.

"They didn't leave out any details, I guess," Emma replied, trying to figure out how she felt about a complete stranger knowing her entire history without ever having met her before.

Maxine leaned towards Emma and patted her on the arm.

"We walk a fine line between neighborly and nosy around here. Don't worry, you'll get used to it."

Maxine turned and headed back through the kitchen as Emma followed, then stopped behind her as they got to the front door.

"That's a beef casserole," she said, pointing back at her dish. "Heat it up for an hour at three-seventy-five or microwave for a few minutes, and it should be enough for a few days' worth of dinner. I figured you hadn't had time to go to the store yet. You aren't a vegetarian, are you?" Maxine asked, squinting at her.

"I'm not. And thank you, I haven't gotten to the store yet, so this is a big help."

Maxine nodded.

"Well, you just bring that dish back whenever you're finished. And come by any time so I can find out about how the new job at the coffee shop is treating you this week," she added with a wink, then pulled the huge door open with her tiny arms, and charged down the driveway and across the street quicker than Emma imagined a woman Maxine's age should be able to move.

As she watched Maxine's departure through her window, Emma tried to remember the interactions she'd had with her neighbors in the decade she lived in San Diego. One downstairs neighbor during college used to come up once a month to tell Emma she was walking too loudly, and one of the neighbors at her townhouse with Blake came by to ask if they'd seen her cat. Aside from that, Emma couldn't think of anyone she spoke to beyond a brief nod or greeting.

But here she was, not even a day into her new life, and the woman across the street knew her name, her history with her ex-boyfriend, and where she worked. And she had brought Emma a casserole. Emma pulled a corner of the foil up from the Maxine's dish, and her stomach growled. If it tasted half as good as it smelled, she'd eat the whole thing by lunchtime.

Maybe having neighbors to talk to wouldn't be so bad, Emma thought, then dug out a large piece and popped it in the microwave.

Emma stopped herself after two large pieces of casserole, and spent the morning unpacking her clothes and toiletries.

Marcy's grandparents kept a fair amount of clothing in the cabin, but had left an entire dresser and the small closet empty for Emma's things.

By four o'clock, the casserole had worn off and Emma was hungry again. She had unpacked all but two boxes, so she called Marcy.

"I told you that you'd sleep through the morning," Marcy said.

"Hello to you, too," Emma said. "But I will have you know I've been up since eight. A nice lady named Maxine came by to deliver a delicious casserole, and let me know that getting dumped would make anybody sleepy."

Marcy laughed. "I'm sorry, I should have warned you."

"That you can't keep a secret?"

"Secret? Emma, two minutes with that woman and she'll know where all the bodies are buried. I dare you to try to keep anything from her. Plus she's sweet and lives alone, and gossip fuels her. And she makes a damn good casserole," Marcy pointed out.

"You've got that right," Emma said, and her stomach growled again just thinking about it. "I'm about to finish it off if I don't leave the premises soon. You up for an early dinner?"

"Perfect timing, I just finished my lesson plans for next week. Do you want me to come pick you up?"

"No, thanks. I want to start figuring out my surroundings. Let me grab a pen and you can give me directions to your house. My reception was pretty spotty on the way out here so I'm not sure how well my phone will be able to guide me."

"Yeah, they only recently put in a cell tower out by Grandpa's place. It isn't very reliable."

"Ah, that makes sense," Emma said as she dug a pen from her purse and took down directions to Marcy's before hanging up the phone. She grabbed her keys and walked out to her car, thinking about who she needed to give her landline number to in case her cell phone didn't work. Marcy already had it, and she could give it to Liz. Blake wouldn't be calling her due to his 'clean break' rule. That left only Maxine.

And she, it turned out, would just show up.

CHAPTER 9

Two hours later, Emma was full of the biggest steak she'd ever seen on one plate, and relaxed after gossiping with Marcy.

"So, tell me about what happened with Blake," Marcy said, signaling the waiter for a refill on their waters. "I know he broke up with you suddenly, but that's about it."

"There isn't much to tell beyond that," Emma said with a shrug, scraping her plate for the last of the mashed potatoes she'd devoured. She would start her diet again tomorrow, she reminded herself as she sucked the fork clean.

"After three years, he decided he was done with me. With us."

"Good riddance," Marcy said.

"I know you didn't think much of him from what I told you, but there were good things. I called you to vent, not talk about how great he was all the time."

"I get that, Emma. It's just, even if things were *good*, it never seemed like there were any *great* things. And it seemed like he made you feel bad about yourself a lot."

Emma sighed as the waiter approached to refill their waters and cleared their plates away.

"I guess at the time, it just felt like Blake was right. He was always working on making himself better, and he just wanted me to be better too. He trains for marathons, and I can barely run two miles without huffing and puffing."

"Emma, he made you feel like eating ice cream was a crime."

"He wasn't that bad," Emma defended, although an image of Blake's raised eyebrows every time she asked for a dessert menu flashed through her mind.

"Plus, I could stand to lose a few pounds."

"Emma, you're barely a size ten. He made you feel like the only thing that would fit you was a circus tent."

"I know, I know," Emma said, using her straw to swirl the ice in her glass.

"You don't know," Marcy argued. "But that's why you're here. I'm going to help you remember what life feels like when you aren't feeling bad about yourself all the time."

Marcy raised her glass.

"To big sky, fresh air, and a fresh outlook," she said, and clinked her glass against Emma's.

"I'll drink to that, even if it's just water," Emma said.

"Now tell me what you know about the internship. I only really know what Don told my mom and me before I convinced you to take it."

"I suspect Maxine knows more about what I'll be doing than I do," Emma said, rolling her eyes.

Marcy laughed. "I wouldn't be surprised. One of the ladies at the magazine lives in your neighborhood, so who knows how much Maxine has been able to pry from her when they see each other."

"I bet she knows what type of toilet paper they stock in the bathroom," Emma joked, although she wasn't sure it was too far from the truth.

Emma took a sip of her drink, then set it back down on the table.

"I don't know much about what I'll be doing day-to-day, but I've been doing my own research along with emailing Don. The magazine itself comes out in paper once a week, but they publish articles online every day. It covers everything happening in Missoula as well as the surrounding towns. Each intern gets paired with a staff member responsible for different sections of the paper."

"Like a mentorship?" Marcy asked, and Emma nodded. "That makes sense. My friend Mark is another writer, and he mostly covers everything related to sports. High school and college football games, even down to sports at the elementary schools. This time of year it's pretty football-heavy though."

"Well I definitely wouldn't be working with him, with my sports knowledge. Or lack thereof," Emma said, thrilled she wouldn't be responsible for covering football games. She had watched with Blake and his friends because they wanted to, but her passing knowledge wouldn't cut it in a magazine read by anyone who knew the game.

"Anyway, it's fifteen hours a week. We have an orientation on Monday morning, then it's every other day for five hours a day. It sounds like I will be in the Features section, mainly stories about local people and businesses, or events. From looking at the website, I think I'll be working with women named Lauren and Jessica."

"Okay, I think I've met them. They're older than us, maybe fifties or sixties. Did Don mention Jason?" Marcy asked.

"Jason? He's the photographer, right?"

Marcy nodded.

"His name is all over the magazine. His photography is amazing," Emma said.

"It is," Marcy said, and a blush crept across her cheeks.

"Are you dating him or something?"

"Ha! No, I just broke up with the fourth grade teacher from my school, remember? I'm not ready to date yet."

"Then what's with the face? Why do you look like you're picturing him in his underwear?"

Marcy touched her cheeks with her palms.

"I'm not making a face," she said, then fanned herself with her napkin. "Anyway, it's nothing, I used to know his brother, that's all. So, do you want to head to a bar after this? I know somewhere we can go dancing."

Emma ignored the change of subject, then gestured to her clothing.

"I'm wearing my moving jeans and a tank top. I hardly think I'm dressed for dancing."

"You're wearing exactly what I am," Marcy said, shaking her head. "Silly California girl, there's more to dancing than shaking your ass and rubbing up against someone. There's a bar in town that has different types of dancing every Saturday. Tonight is either two-step or salsa, I can't remember. Although, what shoes are you wearing?"

Emma stuck her flip-flop covered foot out from under the table, and Marcy grimaced.

"First, we'll go get you some proper shoes. Then we'll go out."

"Marcy, I don't know two-step or salsa or any kind of dancing. I don't think the shoes will be the limiting factor."

"You'll be fine. There's always a mix of people who know what they're doing and novices. Everybody's really understanding. It's just about having a good time."

"Marcy, I really don't-"

"Fresh outlook, remember?" Marcy interrupted. "Let me show you what we have hiding under all this sky."

The image of her new fluffy bed flashed into Emma's head, and maybe a romantic movie on her laptop. But Marcy was right. Emma hadn't moved all the way up to Montana to stay the same girl she was when she left. The move was all about new experiences and figuring herself out, not mourning her old life.

"Okay," she said. "But no cowboy boots."

Marcy just smiled.

Chapter 10

Just before eight o'clock, Emma followed Marcy to the entrance of a small bar in downtown Missoula. She still had on her jeans and tank top, and Marcy had bought her a 'welcome to Montana' gift of brown leather boots. They weren't cowboy boots, but Emma still longed for her flip flops.

Marcy pushed through the door, and Emma's fears of being underdressed were immediately squashed.

In downtown San Diego on a Saturday night, Emma wouldn't have been let into a club wearing what she was wearing now, at least, not the dance clubs Blake took her to. Blake had loved going to the types of places where he could wear his nice shirts and shiny shoes and pay exorbitant prices for watered-down drinks. Emma had tolerated it because she loved Blake, but she had secretly hated spending two hours getting ready to go to a bar where everyone was prettier than her, and she couldn't have a conversation with anyone over the noise.

This bar was not the dark, loud, strobe-light filled club that Emma was used to. And she wasn't underdressed.

There were girls who were dressed up, but there were also girls in jeans and tank tops. Some of the men looked like they had just come from working in their garage, while others wore big hats and buttoned shirts. It was equal parts college bar and local hangout, and Emma felt herself release the breath she'd been holding.

"See? You fit right in," Marcy said, leading Emma through the crowd towards the bar. Looking around, Emma thought that she could have picked any outfit from her closet, and no one who have batted an eye. There was something comforting about that.

"Two Elk Heads," Marcy said loudly to the bartender, who nodded.

"Two what?" Emma said, alarmed, and Marcy laughed.

"Don't worry, it's a beer. Brewed here in Montana, and it's delicious," she said.

"I'm sure it is, but I have to drive home later, and I think it's too far to the cabin to take a cab. Make mine a water," she told the bartender, who nodded. He filled a glass with ice and water before drawing Marcy's beer, then slid both across the counter.

"Keep the change," Marcy said, setting down cash as they took their drinks and stepped away from the bar to let two girls step up and order.

Emma looked beyond the bar to the dance floor that was half-full with a variety of dancers. But like Marcy had mentioned, it wasn't a mass of bodies grinding against each other. Country music played through the speakers as couples moved together around the dance floor, some in simple steps together around the floor, while others worked around their partners in turns and twirls that made Emma dizzy.

"Do you know how to do that?" Emma asked, leaning into Marcy.

"Two-step? I'm learning," she said, her body moving to the beat of the music. "I'm glad it wasn't salsa night. I'm still pretty terrible, but two-step is a little easier to start with. This is the only bar that still has nights for it though. I thought it'd be fun!"

The song ended and changed to one Emma recognized from her drive through Utah.

"Jason Aldean?" she asked, and Marcy stepped back.

"You know this song? I thought you hated country," she said.

"I did. I mean, I do. It was on a lot of the stations during the drive up, so I guess it started to grow on me," she said, still watching the dancers. "Is it difficult?"

"Not at all," Marcy said. "The man does most of the leading anyway, so if you get a good partner, you just need to keep time and keep moving. You'll get the hang of it."

Emma doubted it as she watched a college-aged boy spin his partner in a circle before leading her around the floor with his hand on her back. There was a grace to their movements, an intimacy that somehow dwarfed the simulated humping that most clubs that Blake liked were filled with. Marcy had told Emma that there would be a mixture of experienced and novice dancers, but everyone Emma saw seemed to know what they were doing. She sipped her water and slid her free hand into her pocket, content to watch from a safe distance.

A giant man with arms the size of Emma's face approached, a smile pulling his bearded cheeks up in a way that softened his otherwise intimidating stature. He looked at Marcy and held out his hand.

"Join me for a dance?" he asked.

"I'm actually here with my friend," she said, nodding at Emma.

"No, you go. I'll hold your beer," Emma said, grabbing the glass from Marcy's hand before she could refuse.

"Okay. It looks like that table just opened up," she said, gesturing at the tall bar table behind Emma as she took the giant's hand.

He turned and led Marcy towards the dance floor. Marcy mouthed a quick 'thank you' to Emma before turning around, and Emma laughed. It seemed that Marcy's tastes from college hadn't changed; she still liked them tall, strong, and hairy.

Emma set the drinks on the table and climbed onto one of the stools as she watched Marcy dance across the floor. Her partner was large enough that he probably could have just carried Marcy around, but it looked like she was keeping up with him on her own.

Emma couldn't help but think how Blake would feel about this place. She knew there was a similar club in San Diego, but there was no way he would've ever gone. He would probably hate how underdressed everyone was, or that there wasn't a roped-off area where he could order bottle service.

He would definitely hate the music, Emma thought, smiling as she tapped her foot to a song she didn't recognize. Something about how happiness was as simple as a boat and a good day on a lake. Her smile grew as she tried to picture Blake on a boat, and how happiness would be the furthest thing from how he'd feel.

"Care to share the joke?" a voice said from next to Emma, and she jumped.

"Just daydreaming, I guess," she said, turning her head to face the stranger. She kept her jaw from dropping, but it was difficult.

The man was tall and muscular, not quite the steam engine that was leading Marcy around the dance floor, but certainly well-built. The dark stubble covering his face did nothing to hide his dimples, which were so deep Emma wondered how he ever shaved without cutting himself. His dark hair fell around his ears loosely in a carefree mess, and Emma smelled a hint of cologne emanating from his flannel shirt. It wasn't like the potent brand that Blake usually wore, but something warmer that reminded her of soap.

Maybe it just *is* soap, she thought, mentally slapping herself in the forehead. Not all men felt the need to put on so much cologne that it hovered around them like a swarm of bees.

"Daydreaming, huh? Seems like a strange place for it," he said, raising his beer glass to his lips. His sleeves were rolled up to his elbows, and Emma was mesmerized by the muscles of his forearms that tightened as he moved the glass.

"Just watching the dancers," she stammered.

"Would you like to join them, rather than just watch?" he asked, raising one eyebrow. Emma never realized that eyebrow movement could be so seductive, but somehow this man made it look like an invitation to join him in the backseat of his car.

"I don't really know how, but thanks," Emma said.

But the beautiful stranger just smiled.

"I can tell by the way you're tapping your foot that you can at least keep a beat. I'll do the rest," he said, setting his beer on the table before holding out his hand.

"Also, I'm holding the table," she added.

If there was a more pathetic excuse, she clearly couldn't think of one.

The man pulled the napkins from under her and Marcy's drinks and set them on top of the glasses, then finished the last of his beer before setting the glass down.

"Now people will know we're coming back," he said, smiling at her. He leaned in until the warm smell of clean laundry filled her nostrils, and his hair brushed her cheek.

"Dance with me," he said in a low voice, and Emma nearly melted in her chair.

Emma soon found herself being led onto the dance floor by the tall stranger, her heart pounding in her chest in a combination of lust and terror. He couldn't possibly be attracted to her. He was a gorgeous mountain man, and she felt like pre-transformation Cinderella without a godmother in sight.

As they reached the floor, the man took the hand of Emma's he had been holding and raised it to his shoulder, then took Emma's other hand in his as he lowered his free hand to her waist. She wished she hadn't finished her entire steak and potatoes at dinner, hoping he wouldn't notice that she was testing the tensile strength of her belt.

He smiled down at her, then said, "Ready?" loud enough for her to hear over the music.

Despite how *not* ready she was, Emma nodded, and moved her feet as she felt a push at her waist with one of the man's hands.

Emma knew she stepped on his feet more than once on their first turn around the floor, but as the first song changed into another, she began to get the hang of it. Once she stopped concentrating so hard on her feet and let herself be led, Emma almost began to relax enough to enjoy herself.

She glanced around the dance floor a few times, noticing that a few of the other couples were doing much more difficult moves that involved spinning and occasionally jumping, but others looked just as unsure as Emma felt. Marcy was right that she would have a good time, and that no one would care how bad she was.

The song ended and a new one came on, a slow love song that Emma thought she recognized from her drive, but couldn't remember the singer. She expected the man to step away, but he just repositioned himself and pulled Emma's hand into his chest and reeled her in until her head rested against him. She saw Marcy leaving the dance floor and head towards their table, then look around when she saw it was empty. Just before Emma's partner spun around, Emma caught a glimpse of Marcy's face. Her eyes widened and her jaw dropped, and Emma bit her lip and smiled.

The singer crooned about how he didn't have much money, but he had enough love to keep his wife happy for a lifetime. Emma rested her head against the strong chest at her cheek, thinking about her relationship with Blake.

She believed that she'd loved him, and she had thought she was happy, but she had trouble remembering a time when she had really felt that he loved her. He had given her things, provided for her. As Emma listened to the man in the song describe how he would spend every moment making his beloved feel cared for, Emma fought to keep the tears from falling from her eyes. She thought about Blake, about the gifts he had given her, and found herself wondering if he had ever given her his heart.

In that moment, in a strange bar with a strange man, Emma realized that he hadn't.

The song ended, and Emma pulled her hand from the stranger's own to wipe her eyes before pulling away.

Another man approached as Emma took a step back, and nodded at her before turning to her dance partner.

"Hey man, I've got to head home. I have to report in early tomorrow," he said.

"I'll be right out," her stranger said, and his friend left.

He turned to Emma, his dark green eyes freckled with spots of brown that made Emma feel as though she were looking into a dark forest. He raised her hand to his lips and briefly kissed her fingers. The stubble on his face tickled her, but the warmth of his lips sent a tingle straight down through her new boots into her toes.

"Thank you for the dance," he said, releasing her hand before he turned away.

Emma floated back to the table where Marcy sat, gloating.

"See, I told you it was easy," she said as Emma sat down and pulled the napkin from the top of her glass.

"Hardly. I think I stepped on his feet so many times he'll have bruises for days," Emma said. She took a shaky sip of her water.

"Well, at least it looks like you're ready to get back out there in the dating field," Marcy said, but Emma shook her head.

"No, you were right. I just spent seven years at the wrong job, and three of those years with the wrong man. It's time for me to figure out what's right for me before I go bringing anyone else into the mix. He was gorgeous, and maybe I'll see him again, but for now, I just need to forget about him and focus on me."

"That's going to be tough," Marcy said, smiling as she picked her drink up off the table.

"Why's that?" Emma asked, not liking the way Marcy's eyes gleamed.

"Because *that* was Jason the photographer," Marcy said, pointing at Emma's dance partner.

Emma watched the gorgeous cowboy weave his way through the crowd to the door, then turn back and wink at her just before he disappeared into the night.

"Damnit," Emma cursed, and Marcy choked on her drink as she laughed.

Emma and Marcy finished their drinks, then sat at the bar for a few hours catching up and watching the dancers. Marcy had another couple of drinks and danced with a few other men, but Emma declined the two offers she got. She'd already cried on her future coworker's shoulder, and she didn't need any further embarrassment.

Marcy felt tipsy from her beers, so Emma dropped her off at her house in town before driving the twenty minutes out of town to Marcy's grandparents' cabin. She hadn't yet gotten used to calling it her home yet. It hadn't even been two full days, and technically she would have to move out as soon as it warmed up enough for Marcy's grandparents to come back.

Maxine's porch light was on when Emma drove into her driveway, and while the rest of the house was dark, Emma could have sworn she saw a drape shift in the front window. Emma parked and walked up the porch steps and into the house, throwing the latch shut behind her. Marcy had assured her that she didn't need to lock the house, but Emma hadn't felt comfortable with that just yet.

Emma brushed her teeth and changed into pajamas, then sent an email to Liz describing the cabin and her weekend so far, leaving out the part about dancing with her new coworker. Emma knew that Liz, like Marcy, wasn't too disappointed in Emma's breakup with Blake, and Emma didn't want Liz to get too excited about her meeting someone new.

When she finished, she shut her laptop and grabbed a throw blanket from the couch and her journal, then walked through her bedroom to the back porch. She wrapped the blanket around her and sat on one of the old rockers with her journal in her lap, then looked up through the trees to the sky.

"Wow," she heard herself say.

Missoula itself wasn't a huge city. The population was sixty thousand compared to San Diego's three million, and Emma lived outside of town. So when she looked up, the dark sky was littered with more stars than she had ever imagined could be visible. A cloudy belt that she assumed was a portion of the Milky Way crossed the sky from one horizon to the other, and all of the surrounding space was covered with stars of all different brightness, as though someone had thrown up a huge handful of glitter and all of it had stuck.

The only noises Emma could hear were an owl calling to his mate somewhere in the woods, and the soft trickle of the creek at the back of the property. She took a deep breath and exhaled, thinking that there was nothing in the world in this moment for her to worry about.

Emma opened the book on her lap and strained her eyes in the dark as she flipped to an empty page. She wrote the date at the top, and wrote as well within the lines as she could with such little light.

I wish I could be sure that I've made the right decision.

She shut the book and stared upward, and as she watched, a bright white shooting star streaked across the sky. Emma had never seen a shooting star before, and watched with awe as the trail lingered long after the main source of light had disappeared.

She made a wish in her head just as the last of the light faded, then sat back in her chair and rocked back and forth. The rhythmic creaking of the chair began to lull her to sleep, so she gathered the blanket around her and stood. If sleeping too long in a comfortable bed made her entire body ache, falling asleep in an old wooden rocking chair wouldn't feel good in the morning.

Emma took one last look at the stars at the sliding glass door, wondering how it was possible that so much beauty existed around her every day, and she'd never been aware of it.

She closed the door behind her but left the drapes open. The sun would wake her up early if she didn't shut them, she knew, but she was hoping to see just one more shooting star before she fell asleep.

Emma saw four.

CHAPTER 11

Despite leaving the drapes open, Emma didn't wake up until almost nine the following morning. She heated up another portion of Maxine's delicious beef casserole for breakfast, then spent the morning unpacking the rest of her things and organizing them. At lunchtime she drove into town and pulled up outside of Marcy's small two-bedroom home. Before she could get out of the car, she saw the front door open and Marcy stepped out.

"How's your first Sunday in Montana?" Marcy asked as she slid into the passenger seat.

"Pretty good so far," she said.

"Any good dreams last night?" Marcy asked with a wink.

"If you're asking if I dreamt of Jason, I did not. How about you?"

"Maybe a few," Marcy answered with a grin, and Emma laughed.

"Alright, where are we headed?"

"Go straight, then turn right at the stop sign," Marcy directed. Emma followed her instructions until they pulled into a large parking lot that served a grocery store, department store, and a number of smaller specialty shops. At the end was building painted bright white with 'Mike's Coffee' painted over the door.

Emma pulled into a parking space in front of the shop and turned off the car before stepping out into the warm air.

Around the glass front door were painted images of coffee cups with wings scattered amongst pitchers of milk and curls of steam. Marcy met Emma on the sidewalk and approached the door before opening it for her.

"My savior has arrived!" a voice called through the small shop, and Emma looked up to see Marcy's brother, Mike, wave to them from behind the cash register. He had Marcy's jet black hair and dark eyes, but stood at least a foot taller. He finished ringing up a customer before stepping around the counter to approach Marcy and Emma.

"Good to see you, Mike. And shouldn't I be saying that to you?" Emma asked as Mike gave her a brief hug.

"Not at all. I'm so busy getting the new location set up, I've barely had time to set up interviews. When Marcy called me, it was like fate."

"It's been a long time since I worked at a coffee shop, Mike," Emma said.

"I know, but you'll pick everything right back up. Anyway, if you have a few minutes, I can show you around?"

"That'd be great. I start training tomorrow afternoon?"

"Yes, we have you on the schedule afternoons on Monday, Wednesday, Friday, then opening on Tuesday and Thursday."

"Perfect," Emma said, looking over at Marcy, who smiled at her.

Mike spent ten minutes giving Emma the quick tour of the shop after introducing her to the two college students working that day, and as he pointed out the milk steamers and grinders and presses, she found herself smiling as the memories from working at a coffee shop all through her own college career flooded back to her. The shop itself wasn't all that large; there were just four tables and two couches, but a steady stream of customers came in and out as Mike gave his tour.

Customer bathrooms were just beyond the front lobby down a short hallway. At the end of the hallway, Mike led Marcy and Emma through a door that housed a small employee lounge with a couch, employee bathroom, and short row of lockers for Emma to store her purse or clothing after changing from her internship clothing to the coffee shop uniform - black slacks and a white shirt.

After the tour, Emma took Marcy and Mike out to lunch before dropping Marcy back off at home and driving back out to her cabin. Along the way, her stomach full of something other than casserole and her car filled with groceries, Emma marveled at how much open space there seemed to be everywhere. Her drive from town to the cabin followed a wide, slow-moving river that wound through the hills, each side lined with tall pine trees. In San Diego, beauty like that would be owned and fenced, with giant mansions hidden from view. But there were no homes along this river, and Emma watched the water sparkle as it meandered through the valley in the sunlight.

As she slowed to turn down the road leading to her house, Emma saw an older man stapling a handwritten sign into the telephone pole at the side of the road. He turned as Emma passed, then smiled and nodded before finishing attaching his sign. Emma didn't catch the phone number at the bottom, but she smiled as she read the top of the sign.

'Lost: 3 Cows. If found, please call Dale.'

She shook her head as she drove down the road, thinking that she definitely wasn't in San Diego anymore.

The groceries were all inside the house and Emma was working on packing them away into cupboards and the refrigerator when her cell phone rang in her purse. She answered quickly.

"Liz, hi! So good to hear from you," she said, but Liz's voice came in and out on the other end. "Hold on, Liz, let me call you from the house phone."

Emma hung up her cell phone and looked up Liz's number to dial it on her cordless house phone. Liz picked up after the first ring.

"I could barely hear you, but did you say house phone? I haven't had a house phone since I lived with my parents," she said.

"Yep, the reception is pretty spotty out here in the cabin," Emma explained as she continued putting groceries away.

"Right! You mentioned the cabin in your email," Liz said. "I haven't talked to you in two days, and suddenly I know nothing about your life. Tell me everything," she said, and Emma could hear her friend take a sip of something. Red wine, if Emma knew Liz as well as she thought.

Emma started with the cabin, and once again left out the detail about dancing with the good-looking future coworker at the bar. Liz would have more to say about that than there were hours in the day, and Emma wasn't ready for a pep talk about how she should get herself back out there.

After nearly an hour on the phone, Emma's groceries were put away, and she had caught Liz up enough that she was satisfied. Emma stood at her sink with the phone against her ear, staring out into the woods just beyond, disbelieving that just a week earlier her kitchen view was of a busy road lined with parked cars.

As she watched, a large shape crossed into her field of view. Emma leaned forward and blinked as two more shapes joined the first, walking slowly as they munched on the grass near the creek. When they got close enough that she was sure of what she was seeing, Emma shook her head and laughed.

"Emma? Hello? Are you okay?" Liz asked, but Emma kept laughing. When she finally got a hold of herself, she took a deep breath.

"I'm sorry Liz, I'm going to have to go," she said.

"Is everything okay?" Liz asked.

"It's fine," Emma laughed, grabbing her car keys. "I just need to go call a man about some cows."

CHAPTER 12

Emma awoke early the next morning, an hour before her alarm was set to go off. She had tossed and turned all night in a combination of fear and excitement, hope and regret as she both chided and applauded herself for the sudden change in her life. When the sun began to rise, she had enough of trying to find sleep and got herself up to take a shower.

The bathroom in the cabin was small, and by the height of the ceilings, Emma surmised that Marcy's grandparents must be well shy of six feet. They had built a small loft storage area over the bathroom, so the ceilings in the room were lower than everywhere else, and Emma imagined that someone like Jason would have to slouch if he were to take a shower here.

Emma paused in the middle of scrubbing her hair, wondering where the thought of Jason came from.

Blake was just as tall as Jason, although not as muscular, but he was the one she should have been thinking about in the shower. After all, they'd only broken up a month ago, and she had known him for three years. Jason, on the other hand, was a man she had known for the space of three songs, and they'd barely spoken. And as her future coworker, she shouldn't be thinking about him in the shower. Her shower.

Emma rinsed the soap out of her hair as she decided that thinking about Jason was only a sign that she was beginning to get over Blake, not that she was interested in him romantically.

After repeating that thought to herself ten more times, she finished her shower and stepped out to towel off. She wrapped one towel around her body, and wound another around her hair on top of her head as she walked into the living room. The outfit she'd picked the day before was laid out on the couch, and even though she'd spent an hour deciding on what to wear, she still spent a minute second-guessing herself as she stared at the outfit. She had picked a grey pencil skirt and white blouse, and a green sweater for color. But was it too professional? Not professional enough? Should she wear jeans instead of a skirt, or a jacket instead of a sweater?

After five minutes standing in her towel, she decided to trust the hour she'd spent the day before, and kept moving into the kitchen to start a pot of coffee. As she grabbed the pot and began filling it with water from the sink, she thought she heard the faintest sound from the front porch. Emma turned off the water waited for a few moments, listening, but when the sound didn't come again, she finished filling the pot and poured the water into the coffee maker, then poured the grounds into a filter before switching the pot on. As the coffee brewed, Emma pulled Maxine's casserole from the fridge to heat up one of the last slices for breakfast. She had bought groceries the day before, but starting a new job on just a bowl of yogurt didn't seem like enough.

As she cut a slice and placed it on a plate, Emma heard the sound again. She walked towards the front door, listening. After deciding that she wasn't crazy and imagining things, she slid the wooden plank across the door, trying to keep it centered in the latch so it wouldn't scrape and make too much noise, then pulled the handle to open the door a crack. She peered through the opening just in time to see a small dark cat dart under her porch and out of sight.

Emma stepped onto the porch, calling to the small animal.

"Here, kitty kitty. It's okay."

She tip-toed towards the steps, then down to the dirt. She realized as she crouched that she was still wearing towels and no shoes, but there was no sign of anyone on the quiet road in front of the cabin, so she stayed where she was.

Emma crouched down and peered through the slats of the wooden porch steps, squinting into the darkness under the house, but she couldn't see anything. Remembering the flashlight Marcy's grandparents kept in the kitchen cabinet, Emma trotted into the house to retrieve it, then stepped back to the dirt. Maintaining her dignity in a crouch while wrapped in a towel proved to be difficult, so Emma laid face down on the porch and hung her head over the edge until the towel on her head touched the second step. She flicked on the flashlight and shone it into the dark space beneath the porch, and was met with four pairs of eyes and a chorus of mewling.

"Holy crap!"

At her exclamation, the eyes backed farther away, but Emma was able to get a good enough look to see the large cat and her three tiny babies huddled together in the dirt. One kitten was all black, like her mom, but the other two looked to be a mix of grey and white.

"Hi kitties, it's okay," Emma cooed.

She had always wanted cats, but her mom was allergic, and Blake thought they would be too much trouble. Now she had four underneath her porch. She wondered if they were one of her neighbor's, or just strays, and reminded herself to ask Marcy when she called her later.

"That some new yoga pose?"

Emma dropped the flashlight, and raised her head to see Maxine standing in front of her in the dirt with her arms folded across her dark blue blouse. She had on loose white pants and shoes that matched her shirt, and again wore red lipstick as bright as her hair. Between the two of them, Maxine looked far more prepared to start her day than Emma did.

"No," Emma said, raising herself up onto her knees to pick up the flashlight. She readjusted her towel, then rose to her feet and brushed the dirt from her knees.

"There are four cats under there. Well, one cat and three kittens. Do you know whose they are?"

"Black one?" Maxine said, and Emma nodded. "Little boy down the road had a black cat, but they left it when they moved. Guess she's found herself a home under your porch?"

"Looks that way," Emma said.

"You'll want to get them out before too long or the kittens might turn feral," Maxine said. "Is that what you're wearing to work?" she asked, looking Emma up and down.

"No, I was in the middle of getting ready, but I heard the cats."

Maxine nodded.

"Well, you'll want to look nice for Jason, I imagine. I hear you two make quite the dance team," she said, and Emma furrowed her eyebrows at her.

"How on earth do you know about that?" Emma asked, shaking her head. The woman really did have eyes all over town.

"I have my sources," Maxine said, her green eyes twinkling. "Now go get yourself ready. I'll come by later to help you with the cats, and you can tell me how your first day went. Wait, you have your first day of training at the coffee shop today?"

Emma nodded.

"Tomorrow, then."

With that, the old woman turned on her heel and made her way back down the driveway back towards her house.

Emma shook her head, then stepped back inside the house. If Maxine knew this much about her from third parties, she could only imagine how much the old woman would get out of her after a dinner together. But that was a worry for another day. Because of the cats, she was officially running late.

CHAPTER 13

Emma tried not to speed as she drove down the two-lane road into town, and only noticed the snag in her black tights when she was less than a mile from her new internship. She tugged at her grey skirt while waiting at a light, hoping she could pull it down enough to cover the run, but it was no use.

"Wonderful," she sighed, then jumped when the car behind her honked to alert her the light was green. She threw a hand up in acknowledgement, then pulled through the intersection and down the road.

After two blocks, she pulled into a small parking lot in front of a multi-story red brick building. She drove into an open spot, then glanced at the clock on the dashboard just before switching off the engine.

Seven fifty-five. Still early, assuming she was at the correct address. After checking her reflection in the rearview mirror to make sure her makeup wasn't smudged, Emma grabbed her purse and notebook and got out of the car. She slammed the door, then stared up at the building that housed her new internship, the impetus for her new life.

And she started to panic.

"What am I *doing*?" she whispered to herself, shutting her eyes tight.

Blake's face popped into her head. It was a memory of the time she had showed him the poetry she wrote in her free time, but had never had the courage to show anyone. They'd been together almost two years, and Emma had written a poem about him, and how he made her feel.

And he hadn't gotten it. He'd read it, said, "I don't really like poetry", and had set it down.

She hadn't been able to hide how much it hurt her.

"I'm sorry, I just don't get it. Maybe you just need practice. You know, before I run the marathon..."

And then he'd talked about training for the marathon for an hour. The poem that she'd handwritten onto a small sheet of flowered stationary laid forgotten on the table at his side. He'd set his coffee on it, and Emma remembered watching the wet ring slowly dampen the words until they were nothing but wet ink.

I just don't get it.

She hadn't written anything for him since that day. She had written her feelings for him, and he had set them down. If the person she loved couldn't understand her, then maybe she really wasn't a good writer. So she stuck to her work. She kept at the blog, but the frequency slowed down, as it had with her journal. She stuck mainly to instruction manuals and technical descriptions, the kinds of things she could practice, and get good at. Not poetry, or flowery words, or inspirational pieces for magazines that had no business hiring her.

Blake's face stayed in her mind as tears threatened to push past her closed eyelids.

She couldn't do it. Still fighting tears, Emma fished inside her purse for her keys. Marcy would be mad, but at some point, she'd understand. Liz would probably welcome her back to San Diego with open arms. And Maxine, well, she'd have gossip material for years about the girl who came to Montana and fled before sunset on the third day.

Emma's fingers brushed her keys just as her phone buzzed inside her purse. She reached for it and looked where a text message was waiting.

Good luck on your first day! I know you are going to kick ASS!

Marcy's first text was followed by one filled with hearts and smiley faces, and Emma found herself smiling as well.

Maybe Blake didn't believe in her. Hell, Emma wasn't sure she believed in herself, or even knew who she was these days. But Marcy had faith in her, and today, that would have to be enough.

With what was sure to be the first of many deep breaths for the day, Emma sent a quick text to thank Marcy before dropping her phone back into her purse.

Without giving herself any time to change her mind, she straightened her shoulders and marched to the front of the brick building and through the front doors. The clock on the wall above the building directory rolled into eight o'clock just as she hit the 'Up' button on the elevator.

Just in time to start her new life.

Ready, or not.

Emma knew within seconds of meeting him that she was going to like her new boss, Don.

First of all, he looked at her face when he talked to her, rather than roaming across every other area of her body when he thought she wasn't looking.

Secondly, he reminded her a little of Santa Claus. He was tall with white hair and a matching beard, and a big round belly she imagined he could probably balance a glass of milk on if he tried. Also, he was wearing a bright red shirt, which only served to magnify the resemblance.

First thing that morning, Don held a meeting in a small conference room with Emma and the other two interns, Bev and Corinne, who looked to have just stepped into their twenties. Bev was tall with dark brown hair, but Corinne was shorter with cropped blonde hair. From the way they interacted, Emma assumed they knew each other from college.

After a short introduction and a lot of paperwork, Don started the group on a tour to meet with the team.

"This is our sports writer, Mark," Don said, starting at the office just outside the conference room. "Corinne, you'll mainly be working with him."

"Nice to meet you all," Mark said with a wave. "What do you think of the team's chances this season?"

Corinne shook her head, her hair swishing across the back of her neck. "I think our defense needs work, but the quarterback who just transferred from Florida could take us all the way."

"The sophomore? Not a chance."

"Just wait," Corinne said, and Mark smiled.

"You two can talk shop once we're done with the tour," Don said, then held his arm out to direct them to their next stop. Just beyond Mark's office was a larger shared office. There were desks on either side of a large window, and two women swiveled in their chairs as Don knocked on the open door.

"This is our Features team, Lauren and Jessica. Emma, you'll be working with these two."

"So nice to meet you both," Emma said, shaking each hand while maintaining the smile on her face she couldn't seem to lose.

"You too, Emma," Lauren said. Her hair was a shade of red that reminded Emma of Maxine, although Lauren was sixty to Maxine's eighty. Or ninety. Or two hundred. After just a few meetings, Maxine's energy level had made Emma believe that Maxine would outlive them all.

"They do features on local businesses, as well as research and write up all of the events going on in the area, including the productions the university puts on throughout the year."

"Up until November, when Jessica leaves me to pursue grandmothering full time," Lauren said.

"What can I say? They're too cute to miss a minute of their lives," Jessica answered, and pulled a photo of chubby toddlers from her desk. "They're two and three, and my daughter wants to go back to work part time and could use my help."

"They're adorable," Emma said, and Jessica smiled.

"Well once she's gone, you'll have to come with me to the events we used to do together. The university drama program is incredible. You should join me for their Christmas performance in the winter. It will bring tears to your eyes," Lauren said.

"I'm just retiring, I'm not dead," Jessica said, smacking Lauren on the arm before turning to Emma. "You can come with *both* of us," she said.

"I'll do that, thank you," Emma answered with a laugh, and Don thanked the ladies before gesturing his arm away from their joint office down the hallway.

Emma and the other interns met with Don's assistant and a handful of other people before Emma gave up trying to learn their names, and swore to herself that she would come in early and memorize the name on every door before everyone got in that Wednesday.

As they neared the rear of the building, Emma was sure she had to be getting to the last of the new faces when Don led her into a small window office.

"He's hard to pin down sometimes, but this is our photographer. Jason, these are our fall interns, Bev, Corinne, and Emma."

Emma watched the younger women approach and shake Jason's hand before stepping back. The bubbly, talkative women were suddenly silent, and Emma fought a smile.

"Emma, good to see you again," Jason said, extending his hand.

"You too," she answered.

"You've met?" Don asked.

"My brother and I bumped into her and Marcy this weekend," Jason replied.

Emma glanced at Bev and Corinne, who looked to be star-struck. She couldn't blame them, Jason was good-looking. But he was also their colleague, and after years of being ogled at her own job, she told herself he deserved to be appreciated for more than just his biceps and dimples.

"Jason is the best photographer in the state, and we're lucky to have held onto him for so long," Don said, and Jason blushed as he let go of Emma's hand.

"I believe it. I was looking through the photos on the magazine website, and your name is under almost all of them. You're incredibly talented," Emma said, watching as a light pink brushed Jason's cheeks.

"He actually started as an intern, just like you three," Don said. "He got offers from magazines all over the country, but decided to stay in his own hometown. He can make any picture into a story."

"Thanks, Don," Jason said as he dipped his head in a small bow.

"Only speaking the truth. That's what we do here," he said, turning to the women. "Now let's get you set up in the bullpen."

Emma followed Don out of Jason's office, glancing back to smile at him before she left. The redness in his face had dissipated, replaced by the calm confidence of the man who'd led her around the dance floor. She marveled at how a person so clearly gifted could still be humbled by a simple compliment.

Don walked the three women to a large cubicle just outside his own office that had four desks, one on each wall, each set up with a computer and chair.

"Here we are," Don said. "This is the area we reserve for interns. I think the open-concept allows for better collaboration. Everyone here has an open-door policy, so please come to any of us if you have any questions. If you think you'd like to come in more often than the scheduled three days per week, talk to me, and we'll see what makes sense with your team. For this morning, there is a little more paperwork for you to fill out, and I want you to take some time just reading the magazine to get a feel for the tone, if you haven't already. Go ahead and log onto a computer with the username and password we gave you, and I'll be back in a few minutes."

Emma chose a desk and sat down as Bev and Corinne did the same behind her. She pushed a button on the computer and turned around in her chair as she waited for it to power on.

"This is exciting," Bev said as she turned on her own computer, and Corinne nodded.

"I know. Our first internship, and we get to do it together! Emma, are you excited?"

Emma looked around the cubicle, at the magazine covers pinned up on the walls surrounding them, at the eager smiles of the young, hopeful girls across from her. From across the room, she heard the sound of laughter coming from the direction of Lauren and Jessica's office.

"You have no idea."

CHAPTER 14

After filling out more forms, the interns split up to work more closely with their mentors. In Emma's case, she felt lucky to be paired with Lauren and Jessica. They were friendly, outgoing, and seemed eager to share what they knew. They already had a task for her, which was to look into the background of the university dance team they planned to interview later that week.

At lunchtime, Jessica and Lauren took Emma out to eat, and she got to see more of downtown Missoula. Unlike downtown San Diego, there were no persistent sounds of planes landing overhead or horns honking and echoing off the looming buildings all around.

Now that she thought about it, Emma realized she hadn't noticed any planes since she got there. San Diego had a large military base where jets would occasionally take off and land, and she could hear them periodically regardless of how far away she was. The landing path to the commercial airport was so close to the tops of buildings that Emma held her breath whenever she flew back into San Diego.

In Missoula, there was a constant bustle of cars through the streets during lunch, but it seemed quieter with all the open space around them. From their seats on the patio of the sandwich shop they chose for lunch, Emma could see the river that she had driven by on the way into town. The green hills she could see from her new office were even closer from their lunch spot, and she watched small dots on the hill progress up a trail towards a large "M", for the University of Montana.

After lunch, Emma sat at her desk, researching the university dance team. She felt comfortable with the research aspect of her job, and was so wrapped up in her reading that she jumped in her chair when the alarm on her phone went off. She shut down her computer and raced down to her car to drive to the second part of her new life, training at the coffee shop. She pulled into the parking lot with five minutes to spare, and changed in the shop bathroom from her internship clothes to the coffee shop uniform, white shirt and black pants. As she pulled her hair back, she caught her reflection in the mirror.

She was smiling.

The following day, less than an hour after Emma finished her second day at the coffee shop, Emma found herself in workout clothes on the dirt in front of her house with a can of tuna in her hand, while Maxine watched from the porch.

"So, how was your first day yesterday?" Maxine asked. She held a cup of tea in her hands that she'd brought over, and Emma crouched closer to the porch steps on the ground, holding the tuna that Maxine had also brought.

"It was fine. Great, actually. Lauren and Jessica are really nice, and Don is so easy to work with. His task for the week was basically just to read the magazine. I love the assignment, but I feel a little guilty that my homework is just to read."

Emma peered into the darkness under the porch and thought she made out a few pairs of bright eyes staring back at her. She hoped the cats hadn't been replaced by possums or raccoons in the last day.

"Don knows what he's doing," Maxine said, brushing Emma's concerns away with a wave of her hand. "Besides, it's good to research the magazine so you know what tone to set."

"That's exactly what Don said," Emma said, narrowing her eyes to look up at Maxine, but the woman just dipped her head down for a sip of tea.

Play coy now, Emma thought to herself, but I'll get to your sources soon enough.

"Here, kitty kitty."

Emma leaned forward and spooned a scoop of tuna onto the top step. She continued spooning small amounts in a trail onto the dirt towards herself. She saw the eyes blink at her, but they remained where they were. She set the nearly empty can next to her as she leaned back and crossed her legs.

"So, did you run into Jason at all?" Maxine asked, peering over her cup.

"Your spies didn't tell you that much?"

"Oh they did, but I'd like your perspective," Maxine said with a wink.

Emma snorted.

"I saw him, but only for a second. I don't know why you're reading so much into this. We had one dance, and that was it. Plus I'm still getting over a breakup. I'm not ready for anything new, especially with someone at work." Emma heard herself rambling and bit her lip.

"That's a lot of reasons," Maxine conceded.

"It is," Emma agreed.

"That doesn't mean you can't be friends with Jason. I've known his family for years. His grandmother and I went to high school together."

"Really? And you're still friends?" Emma marveled, and Maxine nodded.

"We are. His whole family is wonderful. He's one of four, and his parents are high school sweethearts."

"Wow, that's impressive," Emma said.

"It is. Those boys have always been the best at anything they try, all of them. Jason in particular with his photography, and I know he does a lot of woodworking in his free time. I remember him taking photos even back when he was a boy, before high school. You could see the focus and determination even from that age, and it stuck with him. He's won a few awards and been published in all kinds of places, but he's still just as kind and humble as anyone. All those boys are."

"They sound like a great family," Emma answered. "His photography is incredible."

"It is," Maxine agreed, taking another sip of tea. "Now, tell me about Blake. From what Marcy told me, he didn't seem all that great."

Emma paused, wondering if it would even be worth trying to delay the conversation, when it seemed Maxine would find out everything sooner or later.

"He wasn't, not at the end at least."

"So why did you stay with him for so long? Three years was it?"

"Just about. And in the beginning it was all good. I was happy, he was sweet."

Emma lowered her voice as she watched a small tongue dart out from the darkness and swipe at the glob of tuna on the step.

"What happened?"

Emma thought for a moment, watching as another tongue joined the first, and she got a small glimpse of grey fluff.

"I guess it's like anything that changes. The good disappeared so slowly that it was hard to notice, like paint fading off a fence. When you see it every day, you don't notice that the brilliant white has become off-white, then nearly brown. But if you leave town for a while and come back, the difference seems so obvious."

Emma shrugged and picked at a lone blade of grass.

"That's how it was with Blake. The good slowly faded away, and it wasn't until recently, now that I've gotten some space and distance, that I can see that the good was gone from our relationship. It probably had been for a while."

Maxine nodded, but said nothing as she sipped her tea. Emma held her breath as the small grey fluff turned into a full kitten that was eagerly lapping up the tuna from the lower step on the porch. A small black fur ball joined the first, and Emma nearly squealed.

"Maxine, they're coming out," she whispered.

Maxine leaned forward in her seat and smiled.

"That's a small litter if it's just the two of them," she said, then leaned back and continued with her tea.

A second grey kitten joined its siblings, and the three of them together teetered on skinny, awkward legs from tuna pile to tuna pile. Their mother crept out from under the comfort of the porch and licked the remnants of the pile farthest from Emma, but didn't come any closer. She sat still just outside the porch as she watched her small litter explore, and Emma was sure she would get a vicious scratching if she tried to get too close.

The kittens were getting closer to Emma, and were within five feet of her, but she remained still so she wouldn't scare them off.

"Well, you'll get over Blake soon enough. And then you can be ready for fresh paint on that fence of yours, whether Jason is the one to put it there or not," Maxine said.

Emma nodded, focused on the little grey kitten that was nearly close enough to touch.

"Still," Maxine continued, "Jason would be a good choice. That boy is sex on a stick."

"Maxine!" Emma shouted, startled, and watched as the surprised kittens fled back to the safety of the porch. Their mother shot Emma a murderous look before joining them, and Emma found herself nearly apologizing to a cat.

Maxine howled with laughter.

CHAPTER 15

It was ten a.m. on Friday morning, and Emma couldn't stop smiling.

At her old job, the only time she ever was even a little happy was on Fridays, because she had a whole weekend of not working to look forward to.

But that day, it wasn't just because it was Friday. For one, after two days of waiting outside her porch, she had finally applied enough tuna and water to get the kittens close enough to pet. After watching her for a few minutes, their mother had even warmed up enough to come and sniff Emma. Once the kittens had discovered that Emma's hands were both a source of comfort and a toy to attack, they hadn't left her side. She'd set up a small box for them on the porch filled with blankets, and planned to get more food and toys for them over the weekend. She'd never had pets before, so she wasn't exactly sure if she could handle four at once, but for now she enjoyed the company.

Secondly, she and Marcy had plans to float down the river that Saturday with some of Marcy's friends. Emma had never floated down a river – the San Diego River wasn't known for its cleanliness – but the way Marcy had described it made it seem like an adventure she couldn't miss before the weather changed and it would be too cold.

But most of all, Emma *loved* her new life. She was still technically training at the coffee shop, but, as Marcy had predicted, making coffee was very much like riding a bike. At first she was afraid that she would feel like being back at a coffee shop would feel like a step back, but throughout the week, Emma began to remember how much she'd actually enjoyed it. She got to interact with different people all day, the majority of whom didn't ogle her, and she got to be on her feet rather than sitting in a chair designed for proper ergonomic function. Mike's shop was busier than Emma had expected, as the proximity to the university made it a popular spot for college students on their way to class or studying. Emma could only imagine how packed the few tables and couches would be once it was time for midterms.

Outside of her paying job, Emma could not believe how much she was already enjoying her internship. She had worked with Lauren and Jessica on what they needed for their upcoming feature, and they invited Emma to come along the following week when they interviewed for the story they were going to publish.

Stories. About people and places and events and thoughts and feelings. She had spent so many years working on a blog no one read, and otherwise tucking away every aspect of writing that didn't have to do with technical facts and details, that she had almost forgotten she was capable of anything else. But she already had events lined up with both Lauren and Jessica the following week and, with their help, she could have an article in the magazine with her name next to it in one of the next issues. She'd been so excited each night after work that Emma had already filled ten pages in her new diary.

She'd been so distracted that she could almost ignore the fact that Blake still hadn't called her. He surely would have found out somehow that she'd moved out of the state, but it was possible he hadn't. She didn't post it on her social media, and Liz wouldn't have told him.

Looking back, she realized how much he had criticized her for not bettering herself by working out more or eating better, how he had been so unsupportive of her dream to be a writer. But here she was, happier than she'd been in years and so far out of her comfort zone she couldn't remember what that zone used to look like.

In her mind, this life change was going to make her better than any amount of running or kale smoothies could have. She wanted him to be impressed, or at the very least surprised. More than likely, Emma had a hard time admitting, he probably just didn't care. But all she could hope was that someday, neither would she.

By the time she needed to leave for her shift at Mike's, Emma was still smiling, but exhausted from the full week balancing work at the coffee shop and the internship. She would be home too late for Maxine to stop by for tea, which she'd done on the two days that Emma didn't have the internship and got home earlier from the coffee shop. Emma wasn't used to someone asking her so many details about her life. Even Blake had done little more than ask about her day by the end of their relationship. But Maxine wanted to know everything short of her second grade teacher's name. At first Emma had found it exhausting, and had given as little information as she could. But she knew over time Maxine would wear her down. Maybe she should just let Maxine read her journal every night just to avoid the evening interviews.

Emma packed her things shut down her computer before leaving her cubicle. She felt her phone buzz in her purse, and looked down as she walked to dig around the large bag for it. Before she could get to it, she felt a warm pair of hands grab her shoulders, and she jumped.

"Whoa there," Jason said, smiling as he held Emma at arm's length.

She'd been so focused on her purse that she had nearly run into Jason as he left his office. Emma had worked through lunch, and was in a rush to grab something before starting her shift at the coffee shop.

"Sorry about that," Emma said, forcing herself to look up at Jason's still smiling face.

"Not a problem," he said, finally letting go of her arms. "You off to lunch?"

"A quick one, then I need to get to the coffee shop."

"Coffee shop?" Jason asked.

Emma nodded. "I work there after I leave here Mondays, Wednesdays, and Fridays until closing, then the early shift on Tuesday and Thursday." Emma checked her phone and realized that she would likely have to just grab a muffin from the shop for lunch. "Well, sorry again for bumping into you. I'll see you Monday," Emma said, starting towards the door.

"Oh hold on, I'm heading out to take some photos. I'll walk you out."

The hallways in the office were narrow, and Emma felt Jason's arm brush hers as they walked next to each other to the elevator.

"How are you liking your first week?" Jason asked as they waited.

It was an older building, which Emma generally loved. The brick exterior was unlike anything in San Diego, since the California earthquake risk limited the use of brick.

But the age also meant that the elevator wasn't incredibly fast, and she listened to it groan as it climbed the shaft to their floor.

Emma looked around the lobby and noticed that one of the bulbs in the floor light was flickering, giving the effect of candles in a light breeze. The area wasn't very large, and she could smell the cologne Jason had used that morning, the same soap-and-sawdust smell she had drank in the night they danced at the bar. She could see the lights reflecting in his eyes as he looked at her, the stubble on his face. She'd spent the whole week without being reminded of her attraction to him, only to be stuck waiting with him for the elevator from the Dark Ages.

"Really great, thanks. The people here are all nice, and Don is just so easy to work for."

"Can't argue with that. I interned with him ten years ago during college, and I loved it so much I came back to work for him when I graduated."

"I don't blame you," Emma replied.

"What was your job before you came here? I thought Don said something about writing, but he didn't go much farther than that."

"I was a technical writer. Mostly manuals for company products, or usage guides for customers."

Emma felt like her last day at work was a year ago rather than a couple of weeks. Everything in her life had changed, from her daily routine to the people she spent time with, and she couldn't believe she had only been here a week.

"That sounds different," Jason said. "What made you leave?"

"I just needed a change, I guess," Emma answered, shrugging.

She only had one friend in San Diego who was interested in her life, Liz, and they saw each other once a month. Now she had Marcy and Maxine, and apparently Jason, all wondering why she did what she did, and how she felt about it. Emma couldn't tell if she liked it or not, but at the very least, it was an adjustment.

The elevator landed at their floor, and the metal doors slowly slid open.

"Well, San Diego to Montana is a change, that's for sure." Jason held his arm out to gesture Emma into the elevator ahead of him, then followed her and pushed the button for the first floor before the doors slid closed behind them. The elevator groaned as it descended, and Emma thought again that she should start taking the stairs, more for her safety than for the exercise.

They rode in silence for the first floor, and Emma focused on counting the flowers on the pattern of the wall behind Jason.

"Why the sudden decision?"

"Hmm?" she asked, losing count.

"To move. I know Marcy is here, but most people would have a hard time with such a big change like that so quickly. Especially on their own."

Emma shifted on her feet. While the elevator ride was long, it didn't seem the appropriate place to delve into her failed relationship and career. Plus she barely knew Jason, and he was just being polite.

"Just felt like the right time, I guess," she said as the elevator slowed to a stop and the doors opened. Again, Jason gestured for her to go ahead of him, then walked ahead of her to the front door and opened it for her.

"Thanks," she said, trying to remember the last time Blake held a door for her.

Strangers did it, sure, but not Blake. He was her first real relationship, so she didn't have a good frame of reference for how most boyfriends behaved. Maybe chivalry was just a kindness for strangers rather than boyfriends and girlfriends.

They walked in silence towards her car, and Emma wondered what else in her own relationship might have been just Blake, rather than all men. That line seemed blurry after being with one man for so long.

She glanced at Jason walking beside her, and wondered what he would be like as a boyfriend. Would he still hold the door for her after the initial magic had worn off, walk her to her car, ask her questions? Not that he would date her, but hypothetically. Would he still be interested in her thoughts, or would he stop being so polite once they were together?'

"I'm not usually so impulsive," she blurted out as they reached her car.

Jason tilted his head.

"The move," she stammered. "I'm not an impulsive person, I just felt like there wasn't anything left staying for. So I left. I know it doesn't sound like a good reason."

"I think that's as good a reason as any," he said.

"I guess," Emma said. "Anyway, thanks for walking me out," she said, unlocking her car.

"Anytime," Jason said, then walked away towards a large black truck on the other side of the nearly empty parking lot.

Emma opened her door and tossed her purse across to the passenger seat before lowering herself down into her own seat. As she reached to close the door behind her, she saw Jason turn around towards her.

"Hey Emma," he called, and she pushed the door open again.

"I'm glad you were impulsive," he said, then turned back towards his truck and hopped inside, then waved at her as he drove past. Emma watched his taillights fade in her rearview mirror as he turned down the road and disappeared.

Her door was still open, and Emma closed it as a light breeze swept through the parking lot. She started her engine and checked her mirrors before she pulled out of the parking lot onto the street.

She felt herself smile as she debated how long to wait before telling Maxine.

CHAPTER 16

The next morning, Emma found herself standing in front of the full-length mirror in her bedroom with two of her new kittens swirling around her feet, wondering if Marcy was more likely to believe a food poisoning story or a sore throat.

Emma sighed and tightened the strap around her neck, then shifted herself around in the top half of her two-piece bathing suit, wondering if there might be a tarp hiding somewhere that she could wear instead.

She'd had the bathing suit for over a year, but had never worn it. She bought it when she thought she and Blake were going to Hawaii for a vacation, but his job had gotten too busy to take any time off, and they'd had to cancel. At the time, Emma had been disappointed not to spend the time with Blake, but also relieved that she wouldn't have to spend a week in a bathing suit. Even with Blake, she was rarely naked with the lights on.

Which, as she stared at herself in front of the mirror, was a thought that made her equally depressed and furious. When had she decided that her own boyfriend wouldn't want to see her naked? The farther she was from the relationship, the more Emma wondered what had made her think that was what happiness felt like.

But it was over. She still thought about Blake, still woke up at night going over how she could've missed the decline of their relationship, but each night she was awake less, and thought about him less.

Her issue of the day was not Blake-related, but rather the issue of spending a day in a bathing suit in front of strangers, something she hadn't done since college. Even then, she couldn't remember taking off her cover-up for longer than a half hour or so. Which was why she was trying to come up with a convincing lie to tell Marcy that would get her out of the float down the river, but wasn't so dire that Marcy thought Emma needed her to come over.

As Emma settled on a low-grade fever, the cordless phone rang.

"Hello?"

"Shouldn't you be heading down to the river?"

Emma frowned and walked to her window. She pulled back the shade and saw Maxine sitting on her front porch with a cup in one hand, the other holding the phone to her ear.

"I'm not sure I'm feeling well," Emma lied, dropping the shade in case Maxine's eyes were as good as her intuition.

"Mmhmm," Maxine said, and Emma heard her take a sip of tea. "You seemed to be feeling well enough on Thursday night."

Emma sighed.

"It snuck up on me, I guess," she said, then threw in a small cough for effect. Even to her ears, it sounded fake.

"A lot of things will sneak up on you," Maxine said. "Old age is one of them, I can say from experience."

Emma could feel the weight of Maxine's guilt trip even with the shades closed, and sighed again.

"I just don't know if I'm up for it," she said.

"I know," Maxine answered. "A lot of things can be new and scary, but that doesn't mean they aren't worth doing. I've lived a long time, and I plan to live a while longer yet. And let me tell you, I'm not sitting out here on this porch reminiscing about all the times I stayed inside and hid. I'm thinking about all the times I didn't."

Emma walked back to the mirror with her phone in her hand and looked at herself again. Today wasn't about how she looked in a bikini. Today, and the whole idea behind moving to Montana, was about being brave enough to find out who she was supposed to be.

"Thanks, Maxine," she said.

"Sure thing. Don't forget your sunscreen."

Emma left a dry change of clothes in her trunk along with a towel, then slammed the lid shut and walked from the spot next to the road where she'd parked down to a small group of people at the edge of the water. She wore a black crochet cover-up dress over her bathing suit that she planned to discard as soon as she was submerged. Marcy waved as soon as she saw Emma, then ran up and gave her a hug.

"I was afraid you weren't coming!"

"I just got a little hung up at home," Emma said, hugging her back. "I wasn't sure what to bring, so I have some bottles of water and cans of beer. And sunscreen," she added, mentally thanking Maxine as she felt the warm sun already trying to burn the tip of her nose.

"That's perfect. Bring it down here. We have a floating cooler so we'll just throw these in there. Come meet everyone! They're so excited to meet you."

Emma took a deep breath as she followed Marcy down to the group of people standing around the cooler. There were two men about her age, and another woman.

"Everyone, this is my friend Emma who just moved here a week ago. Emma, this is Pete, Jamie, and her husband Matt. Jamie and I work together at the elementary school."

Emma shook hands with everyone, and was unsurprised to find how friendly they all were. She was usually nervous in situations where she didn't know everyone, but, like almost everyone else she'd met since she moved to town, Marcy's friends seemed to have a limitless supply of questions. Within ten minutes, Emma had told them all about San Diego, her job, and enough about Blake that they were all united in their hatred for him.

Emma was surprised how open she was with them, and impressed with how inquisitive they were. As they moved onto the subject of the river height and temperature, Emma wondered if they'd gone to the same school as Maxine in 'how to interrogate a stranger in ten minutes', or if the friendliness was just natural in this part of the country.

As the others talked, Emma checked out the rafts. She counted seven black donut-shaped tubes.

"Are the extra two just in case one of ours pops?" she asked, hoping the water was as slow-moving downriver as it seemed to be where they stood.

"No, the car tire tubes almost never pop. Those are for Jeff and Jason," Jamie answered. "They had to drop Jason's truck off at the access point of the river we'll be getting out at so we could get a ride back up to our cars," Jamie explained.

"Jason?" Emma looked at Marcy, who was picking a loose thread on her cover-up.

Emma was about to press Marcy again when a loud truck pulled in above them along the road. The engine turned off, and Emma saw Jason inside the cab.

She watched him hop out, and noticed even from this distance that his calves appeared just as firm as his forearms. He was wearing swim trunks and a tank top, giving Emma her first glance at his biceps, which were impossibly big and so well-defined that they created their own shadows on his arm. The man with him was also in incredible shape, and even larger than Jason, but Emma couldn't take her eyes from the photographer.

As they approached, the men greeted the rest of the group, and Jason's eyes finally landed on Emma. She regretted her decision to not have a fever, knowing that his reaction to her body could not come close to how she felt when she looked at him.

Jason smiled and patted Jeff on the back.

"This is my older brother, Jeff," he said, and the giant extended his hand.

"Nice to meet you finally," Jeff said, shaking Emma's hand. "I saw you at the bar last week, the night you two danced. Nice to put a name to the face."

Emma felt herself blush as she glanced at Jason, then shook Jeff's enormous hand.

"I don't know that you could call it dancing. It was mostly just Jason leading me around while I tried not to trample him to death."

Jeff threw his head back, laughing. "Sweetheart, you couldn't trample him if you tried. That'd be like a mouse taking down a mountain lion."

Jeff kept laughing as he grabbed a beer from the cooler, and leaned down to give Marcy a hug. Emma couldn't help but notice her friend's eyes light up over Jeff's shoulder as she received his enormous embrace, and she reminded herself to bring it up with Marcy when they were alone.

"A mouse and a mountain lion?" Emma repeated to Jason, still watching Marcy's face grow with excitement as Jeff pulled away and they started a conversation.

"Well, yeah," Jason said.

"Because of my nose?" she guessed.

"Your nose?"

"Yeah, my dad used to say my nose was too small for my face," Emma said, immediately wishing she hadn't. She'd just invited Jason to scrutinize her face in a way she definitely wasn't comfortable with.

"It's not your nose," he said, laughing. "He just means, you're entirely too small to trample someone like me. You're a perfect size for a dance partner. You stepped on my toes at least twice and I barely felt it," he added with a wink.

"You said I wasn't bad!" Emma smacked him on his arm, noticing that it was just as large and hard as it looked. Which made her wonder what else on him was large. And hard. She felt her heart race and the heat rise in her face again at the thought.

"I'm pretty sure all I said was 'thank you for the dance'," he returned.

Before Emma could answer, Pete told everyone to pick a raft, and Jason turned away towards the river.

It gave her time to think about what he'd said about her. He didn't tell her that if she just worked out more, her bathing suit would fit better, or that if she skipped dessert she could probably get down to a size eight. He called her small.

Blake used to joke that she was 'pretty, but everyone needs improvement', his not-so-subtle way of telling her she needed to lose weight to be considered pretty. Around Blake, she realized, she felt as though she was always one workout away from him loving her the way she wanted to be loved. She was one diet away from a proposal.

But Jason just told her she couldn't hurt him if she tried, because she was a perfect size.

Shaking her head, Emma followed him to the rafts. Jason held out a raft for her before grabbing one for himself.

"Ready?" Marcy asked, her own face as flushed as Emma was sure hers had to be.

"I have no idea," Emma responded, and walked into the river.

Two hours and two beers later, Emma had learned that Matt and Jamie were expecting a baby, Pete and Jeff were both firefighters, and Marcy had a crush on Jeff that was growing larger and less inhibited with every turn in the river.

Emma had also discovered that Jason's chest and back muscles, like the other parts of him she'd already seen, looked to have been chiseled from smooth marble. She planned to either leave her cover-up on, or lay it across her stomach as they floated, but Jamie had offered to put it in a dry bag for her, and since everyone else had already put their clothing in, Emma felt that she shouldn't be the odd-one-out by refusing. At first, she tried to keep most of her body submerged beneath the raft, holding her feet up to avoid hitting any rocks on the bottom and trying not to shiver. But after the two beers and a number of stories from Jeff and Pete about the entertaining side of living with ten men in a small firehouse, Emma had all but forgotten her earlier insecurities. She was just having too much fun, and rode on top of her raft where the sun could warm her body.

It was also nice to get to know Jason as more than the hot photographer she shared a dance with. She'd found herself floating next to him more often than not, and she'd learned more about his life as one of four brother. She also found out that he owned a small cabin outside of Missoula that he had built himself.

Jeff had cut in to tell Emma about all of the tables and shelves and bed frames Jason had built over the years and how good he was with his hands, compliments that had put a light blush on Jason's face. Emma couldn't help but picture Jason, shirtless and sweaty, gently sanding down a bedframe.

In reality, it was unlikely that Jason did his woodworking shirtless, but it made for a nice fantasy.

At almost two in the afternoon, the group rounded the final bend to where Jason had parked his truck. As Jason and his brother deflated the rafts, Emma dried herself off with a towel Jamie provided and quickly threw her cover back on. Marcy, in the other hand, stood tall in just her bathing suit, dripping as she watched Jeff bend down over a raft and push the air out.

"So," Emma said as Jeff and Jason piled the empty rafts and carried them up to Jason's truck.

"Hmm?" Marcy answered, still staring at the elder brother.

"So, you didn't tell me Jason was coming."

"Right," Marcy said, pulling her gaze from Jeff to look at Emma. "I'm so sorry, I didn't plan on him coming. I ran into Jeff yesterday at the grocery store, and the invitation just slipped out of my mouth. I don't see him much these days, but I had a huge crush on him in high school."

"You don't say," Emma said.

"Is it that obvious?"

"I think Matt and Jamie's unborn child could see it," Emma said. "Although I'm glad to see you're over your breakup."

"Oh, definitely over it," Marcy said, her eyes floating back to Jeff as he dried his hair with a towel before tossing it to Jason.

Emma watched his biceps flex as he ran the towel through his hair. The strands were still damp, and he ran his fingers through it to pull the strays from his eyes.

"And how about you? Any progress in getting over Blake?" Marcy asked, and Emma turned to see that her staring hadn't gone unnoticed.

"It's only been a month. I'm not ready for anything," Emma protested. But her resolve had faltered over the past week. Between her new house, new job, and new pets, Emma realized how quickly her life could change. Maybe her feelings weren't far behind.

"Even if I was, I don't even know if he's single. And I work with him."

"One, you can just ask him if he's single. And so what if you work with him?"

"So, if we broke up, it would be awkward."

"Not necessarily. The teacher I dated still works at my school, and things are normal between us. Plus, who's to say you'd break up?"

Emma looked back up at Jason and imagined what it would be like to have his arms around her again, feel his stubble against her face, and shook her head.

"Why are we talking about this? There isn't a chance. He's gorgeous, a fantastic photographer, and apparently a woodworking genius. And a gentleman."

"And?" Marcy asked.

"And I'm a recently-dumped technical writer who works at a coffee shop and may or may not be an actual writer, who needs to work out more and eat less. I'm just a mess."

Marcy furrowed her eyebrows at Emma and shook her head.

"Someday, you're going to tell me who put all that darkness in your head."

Before Emma could respond, Pete and Matt walked up.

"Ready to head back to the cars?"

Marcy nodded, and Emma followed them all up to Jason's truck. At Jason's insistence, the men all piled in the back of the truck, and the three women piled into the cab. Marcy and Jamie jumped into the small seat in the back of the cab, leaving Emma the seat next to Jason.

Even though the float down the river had taken nearly three hours, the drive back to their cars only took twenty minutes. But sitting next to Jason, trying to make small talk while pretending she didn't want to lick every drop of water falling from his hair to his shoulders, made the drive feel like an eternity.

When they made it back to their cars, Pete, Matt, and Jamie rode away together, and Jamie left promising to invite Emma to the next girls' night she had planned. Marcy had had too many beers to drive, so Jeff offered to drive her home.

Jason waited in his truck while Emma approached her car and opened the trunk. She stepped behind the open trunk and pulled her damp cover-up off her body and replaced it with a large dry sweatshirt that felt warm and comfortable after sitting in her trunk in the sun for the last few hours. She grabbed her purse and closed the trunk, then fumbled inside to check her phone as she headed towards the drivers' door. Emma turned on the phone and saw two text messages.

One was from Liz asking how her day was going, and the other was from Blake.

Emma debated just deleting it without reading it, then wondered whether or not she could throw her phone into the river at this distance.

Finally, curiosity got the better of her and she opened the message. Maybe he couldn't make as clean a break as he thought. Maybe he missed her.

Hey, got our deposit back from the apartment. Send me your address and I'll mail you your half.

Emma stood staring at her phone outside her car, listening to the river and wishing she'd gone with tossing the phone.

"Hey, you okay?'

Emma looked up across her car and noticed that Jason hadn't left yet and was watching her from his truck.

"Fine, sorry," she called, waving as she fumbled her keys into the lock in her car door. In her haste, she dropped her keys into the grass, and dropped her purse when she went for her keys, sending the contents tumbling.

Emma got to her knees in the grass and grabbed her phone, then heard a car door slam as Jason approached. She tried to focus on gathering her belongings and putting them back into her purse, but she felt the rage and frustration bubbling just beneath the surface.

"Are you sure you're alright?" Jason asked from above her, and Emma finished packing up her purse before she stood up and sighed.

"I'm just annoyed, that's all," she said, staring out at the trees swaying in the breeze. "And I'm even more frustrated to be annoyed in such a beautiful place."

"You've lost me," Jason said.

Emma turned and unlocked her car, then tossed her purse inside before slamming the door.

"Really, it's fine," she said, but Jason didn't move.

"I only have brothers, but I've found that usually when a woman says she's fine, she isn't. She just hasn't worked out exactly how to say what's bothering her."

Emma sighed.

"I'm bothered, but it's nothing I need to bother *you* with," she said.

"Try me," Jason said, then walked to the front of her car and leaned against the hood. He looked back at her and patted a spot next to him.

Emma debated for a moment, then shut the door and joined him on the hood. She watched the river, wondering how just hours ago she had been willing to believe she was already on her way to being over Blake. One text message proved her very, very wrong.

"Three years," she said finally, and Jason turned to look at her. "I was with my boyfriend for three years, and he just... ended it."

Jason nodded but didn't respond.

"I left without telling him where I was going. I haven't heard from him in a month. He dumped me, left the apartment, and I haven't heard from him since. He doesn't even know I'm here. He doesn't even care. Then he sends me a message asking for my address so he can send me a deposit check, and that's it. No 'how are you?' or 'what's new?'. Just business. Like I was anybody, not his girlfriend. Sorry, ex-girlfriend," Emma corrected.

Emma took a deep breath as she watched the river glide between the banks in front of them. A breeze rustled the leaves between the trees, and Emma folded her arms tighter across her chest.

"And it's so frustrating because I don't think I should need validation from anyone that I've made the right choice, that leaving a stable job to work at a coffee shop and an internship wasn't incredibly insane. And maybe it isn't the validation I need, maybe I just want him to care? I don't know."

"I get that," Jason said, nodding. "It was a long relationship. You want the other person to be as affected by the end of it as you are, otherwise it feels like you weren't in the same relationship."

"I think that's part of it," Emma answered. "I think part of me just wants him to realize that I don't need him, that I could move on as easily as he did."

"Is that why you moved up here? To prove a point to him?"

Emma took a deep breath, then shook her head.

"I moved because I was stuck. From reading through my journal, I wasn't as happy as I thought I was with Blake. And I definitely wasn't happy in my job."

"You didn't try to get any writing jobs down there?"

"I applied to a few magazines and journals before I got the job as a technical writer, and then I kept telling myself that if I kept writing my blog, something would happen. When Marcy called, I realized that something wasn't going to just 'happen'. I had to make a choice. The rut I was stuck in was bigger than just the job and the relationship, it was a whole mindset. I think I needed a change this big to snap myself out of it."

Emma turned to Jason and saw that he was staring at her, his eyes boring into hers. She blinked, then turned back to the river, breaking their connection.

"But I guess I haven't come as far as I thought, since apparently one text from an ex can send me into a whirlwind of doubt."

Emma sighed, then turned back to Jason, who was still staring as though she had grass on her face.

"What?" she asked, wiping her cheeks.

"Sorry, it's just," Jason paused, tilting his head. "You took one of the biggest risks anyone could ever make. You left an entire life to take a chance on yourself, on your own happiness. You're working a full-time job and an internship. And on top of that, you have Maxine as a neighbor," he added, and Emma smiled. "You said that you and Blake only broke up, what, a month ago?"

"Just about," Emma said, nodding.

"I just think you need to give yourself a break. After three years, I'd be surprised if you didn't want someone who was supposed to love you to care about what you're up to a month after you broke up. It sucks that he's acting like he doesn't care, but if that's the kind of guy he is, you're probably better off."

Emma felt her cheeks warm with Jason's compliments, and she bit her lip as she looked over at him. The sun was behind the trees, and the shafts of light passing through the leaves and branches threw shadows onto Jason's face.

"And I know you barely know me," Jason added, "but if it's any consolation, I'm impressed as hell."

"Thank you," Emma whispered. She looked into Jason's kind face as he smiled, his dimple creasing his cheek and his eyes crinkling at the sides. They both looked back to the river, listening to the breeze through the trees and watching the river flow by.

"You don't have to keep sitting here with me," Emma said after a few minutes of peaceful silence.

"Do you want me to go?"

"No, I just meant that if you have anywhere to be, don't feel obligated to stay."

Jason smiled again, and Emma couldn't help but smile back.

"I've got nothing but time. I'm enjoying getting to know you."

"Me too," Emma said. "Although I think this has mostly been a one-way conversation where you get to know a lot about me, and then stroke my ego. I don't know anything about you."

"Fair enough," Jason laughed. "To be fair, I wasn't just stroking your ego, I was being honest. But what would you like to know?"

Emma twisted her mouth, thinking, before sitting up straighter. "Okay. Since you got to see a part of my relationship, how about yours?"

"My what?" he asked, leaning towards her.

Emma held her breath, but his intoxicating scent still made its way into her nose, and she felt her heart beat faster. She only hoped he couldn't hear it.

"Your love life. You've already learned about my failed relationship, so tell me about what's going on with you?" she stammered, hoping her face wasn't turning red. She shouldn't have asked him anything, she thought.

Jason shrugged.

"No love life," he said, and Emma scoffed. "That's a surprise to you?"

Emma shook her head. "It's just, you're so…" she trailed off as she felt the blush creep up her cheeks. "So charming. And successful," she said. "Your photography is authentic and moving. You can tell how passionate you are just looking at your photos."

Jason leaned back, and Emma took a deep breath of fresh air. He stared at her for a moment with a strange half-smile on his face that Emma couldn't decipher.

"I guess I just haven't found the right girl," he said.

"You're not into flings?" Emma asked.

"Are you?" he countered.

"No," she answered. "I didn't really date in college, and my only real relationship was Blake. It turns out I might not be so great at quality, but I don't think quantity is the answer."

"Well, it takes two people to succeed in a relationship, so I don't think you can take all the blame for the quality."

"I guess," Emma said, staring out at the river.

It was such a peaceful spot, sitting on her hood next to Jason while the river meandered by. She could almost forget about Blake and the pain he had caused her. She could learn to trust again, she knew that. But would it be worth it?

"So you're not into flings," she said, still staring at the river. "What are you looking for?"

Emma waited while Jason leaned on the car next to her, and she wondered if she'd gotten too personal. She was about to apologize when he started to talk.

"I've had a few relationships, some just a couple months, and the longest was two years. But now that I'm thirty, I'm looking for that thing I see in every perfect picture I take," he said. "That spark of truth that turns the photo into a story and makes you feel something when you look at it. I'm looking for that spark in someone else, someone who makes me see the world in a way I hadn't considered. Someone who inspires me. I'm looking for big, real love."

Emma sat speechless, listening to the breeze and wondering how to respond. She had never known a man to open his heart in such a way, except in the romantic movies she watched late at night on her laptop. She always cried at those parts, knowing that such a man didn't exist.

"You think we're even in the 'getting to know each other' territory?" Jason asked, and Emma looked at him just in time to see him wink at her.

"I think we are," she answered. "And it looks like it's getting late, so I should probably get home before Maxine starts calling me."

"So, you two are getting close?" he asked, sliding off the hood and offering Emma his hand so she could do the same.

"Despite my best efforts," Emma replied, and Jason laughed.

"Yeah, Maxine's a riot," he said, then waited for Emma to get into her car before walking to his own.

Emma turned her key in the ignition and was about to pull out when she saw Jason waving to her from his truck. She rolled down the window and leaned over the passenger seat to see him.

"You're gonna be just fine, Emma Ward," he said, then backed up his truck and pulled onto the highway.

She fastened her seat belt and put her car into reverse and turned around in her seat to check behind her before backing up onto the road.

Good-looking, kind, and talented, Emma thought. He was definitely going to put her 'no dating' goal to the test.

CHAPTER 17

"And then what?"

The following evening, Maxine sat in her spot in the chair on Emma's front porch while Emma played with the kittens on the porch floor. The kittens' mother, who Emma had named Daisy, sat at the edge of the porch staring towards the fading light of the sun as it crept towards the horizon.

"And then nothing. He went home, I went home."

Emma flicked the stick in her hand to make the attached string dance across the porch, and smiled as the kittens all bounced in a clumsy attack.

"No kiss?"

"What?" Emma exclaimed, dropping the stick and sending all the kittens scurrying.

"I know he's a gentleman, but I don't think one kiss would be out of the question."

"Why would he kiss me?" Emma asked. "We were just sitting together, talking. And we were mostly talking about Blake, so it definitely wasn't a date. He's not even interested. I've known him a week, and we're coworkers."

"That's a lot of commentary for something that didn't happen," Maxine mused, and Emma leaned forward to pick up the cat toy again. "Let's put aside all the 'why he wouldn'ts' for a minute. What do you think about Jason?"

"You know what I think about him," Emma said.

"No, I know what you think about relationships. You said you aren't ready. I don't know anything about what you think about Jason."

"Why are you so interested?"

"My television is broken," Maxine answered.

Emma sighed.

"I think that he's an incredible photographer. His ability and clear passion is clear just from looking through the magazine. Obviously, he's attractive," she said, and Maxine snorted. "Fine, he's gorgeous. And he seems so close with his brothers, which I envy a little because I'm an only child."

Emma watched her kittens play with each other and wondered if they would always be as sweet and close to each other as they grew older.

"He's a gentleman, and he's kind and inquisitive without being pushy."

"And?"

"There is no 'and', Maxine. He's still my coworker, he's still so far out of my league we may as well be on different planets. And I'm still not ready, even if he wasn't all of those things."

"Hmm."

Maxine sipped her tea in a rare stretch of silence while Emma played with the kittens until the sun set. Emma had heard coyotes the night before and decided to keep the cats inside at night, so she went into the kitchen and filled their bowls with cat food to coax them into the safety of the kitchen. The kittens were easy, but their mother would only come inside for fresh cat food.

Emma went back out to the porch and sat on the edge, watching the pink and orange horizon light up the sky behind the tall trees at the edge of her property.

"It's fine not to be ready," Maxine said, breaking the silence, and Emma turned to face her. "And it's fine to mourn the end of something. Just be careful to let it go when the time is right, and not just hold on because you're afraid of what you might come next."

Emma nodded as Maxine rose from her chair. She patted Emma on the shoulder as she shuffled past her on the porch steps, and Emma watched as she retreated towards the road with her empty mug in her hand.

"Oh, wait!" Emma darted inside and grabbed Maxine's dish from the drying rack next to the sink, then trotted back out to meet her on the path. "Your dish," Emma said, holding it out. Maxine stared at it for a moment before taking it, and Emma wondered if she should have offered to carry it for her.

"Hmm," was all Maxine said before turning back to the road.

CHAPTER 18

"I talked to the coach. Practice ends in about ten minutes, and she'll let the girls know we're here, so we should be able to talk to the ones who don't have class right away."

It was Monday, just before lunch, and Emma sat beside Lauren and Jessica in the university basketball stadium watching the dance team practice for a competition that was two weeks away. Emma felt incredibly lucky to work with such capable and friendly mentors. Jessica had been a writer for magazines or newspapers since she graduated college, and had worked for Don for at least twenty years.

Lauren was just as experienced, and had even published a handful of children's books in her spare time. Both women had been more than willing to help Emma feel comfortable asking questions, and their openness helped her feel less concerned about her own inexperience. If there really was such a thing as a fairy godmother, Emma believed she'd just found two.

Three, if she counted Maxine.

"So, are we doing an article on the team, or their upcoming   event?"

"Both," Lauren and Jessica said in unison, and Lauren laughed before gesturing to Jessica.

"We want to write up the team and their practice today to entice people to attend their event. By giving our audience a glimpse into the team, the girls working so hard here, it personalizes the event."

"It makes people feel like they'd be rooting for someone they know rather than just 'some college kid,' so they're more likely to show up," Lauren added. "Plus, the coach said that a number of girls are graduating this year, so she's hoping to get the word out to current or potential students who might be interested in joining."

Emma nodded before turning back to watch the team. Three girls in front each did a backflip in place, while the group around them twirled in circles like ballerinas. The music ended, and each girl froze in their own final pose. Emma clapped along with Jessica and Lauren, and a few of the dancers gave them a quick nod before their coach headed over.

Emma couldn't hear the coach's comments from where she sat, but it seemed mostly positive, based on the small smiles and vigorous nods of the young dancers. After a few minutes, all but four girls trotted away, likely to change for class, and the coach waved Jessica and Lauren over.

Emma followed closely with her notepad, her heart beating like a bass drum in her ears. It was her first real interview, and she found her legs were shaking as she walked towards the smiling group of dancers and their coach. They could have been a firing squad rather than a group of cheerful dancers with how nervous Emma felt.

"Beautiful job, ladies. Really wonderful," Lauren said, smiling, and introduced herself, along with Jessica and Emma, to the team and their coach.

"How on earth do you flip around like that? I get dizzy just standing up too fast," Jessica said to Melissa, one of the most acrobatic of the group.

"Lots of practice, I guess," she answered with a shrug.

"We practice three times a week as a group," the coach supplied as the girls stood tall behind her. "Up to six or seven if we have a competition coming up, like the one next week."

"That's a lot to keep up with," Lauren said to the dancers. "How do you balance that with school and a social life?"

The girls shrugged, almost in unison, and Emma wondered how their bodies could move with so much grace and strength with background music, but somehow now were reduced to just shoulder movements.

"There is a GPA threshold the girls need to meet in order to stay on the team," the coach said, taking the lead in the young women's silence. "We encourage focus on the team, of course, but academics always comes first."

"Coach Sterling," Jessica interjected, "would you mind sitting on the bleachers with me so I can get the details we should highlight for the competition? Lauren can stay here and talk to the girls, but I need to sit down. These knees aren't what they used to be."

"Of course," said the coach, who led Jessica back towards the bleachers and out of earshot. Emma thought she caught a look between Jessica and Lauren as Jessica departed, but Emma couldn't be sure.

"That's a lovely necklace," Lauren said to the most petite dancer, Lydia.

The necklace was a small gold ballerina on a gold chain, and Lydia reached her hand to her neck to finger the necklace as she replied.

"Thank you," she said with a smile. "My mom got it for me when I first got into dance. Ballet."

"It's beautiful," Lauren said, her smile soft and genuine. "How long ago was that?"

"I was eight, so almost twelve years. The chain has broken a few times, but I just move the charm onto another chain."

"How about you, Grace? Was it ballet for you as well?"

Grace, the tallest of the four with them, shook her head.

"My grandparents are from Ireland, so I started with Irish dancing when I was six or seven. I moved onto ballet and then more modern dance as I went through high school."

"Same here," Melissa supplied. "The ballet and modern, not the Irish dance. I started with tap when I was five."

"Wow, only five?" Lauren asked.

"Don't be too impressed," said Alice, who stood just next to Melissa. "She was awful. She made so much noise that my dad 'lost' her tap shoes one day and she had to switch to ballet."

Emma watched as Melissa nudged Alice, and noticed a similarity in their features she hadn't seen before.

"Sisters, how wonderful!" Lauren exclaimed, and the girls all smiled.

Emma watched as Lauren continued asking questions, and the dancers visibly became more relaxed and animated. After another ten minutes, Coach Sterling and Jessica made their way back to the group.

"I think I have everything I need," Jessica said to Lauren. "How about you?"

"All set," she answered before turning to the coach and dancers. "Thanks so much for your time. We'll send you a proof of the article before we print it to make sure we get all the details correct."

"Thank you for coming by, and for the support," Coach Sterling answered.

"Good luck, ladies!" Jessica said, and the girls thanked her before following their coach back to the locker room.

"I'm starving. Let's get lunch," Lauren said, and Jessica agreed.

Fifteen minutes later, Emma was sitting across from her new mentors as they shared a fried cheese appetizer and waited for their entrees.

"So what was that all about? Separating the coach from the team?" Emma asked.

Jessica finished chewing and took a sip of her soda before answering. "The coach is their leader. They have their personalities on their own, but in that room, with their leader in front of them, they look to her for guidance."

"Combine that with the fact that they have a competition coming up. That's probably all any of them will be thinking about until after it's over, so removing their coach helps them to get out of that zone for a minute."

"Genius," Emma mused, and the two older women laughed.

"I don't think anyone's ever called me that before," Lauren said.

"Speak for yourself," Jessica answered, and Lauren nudged her.

The waitress brought their entrees, salads for Emma and Lauren, and pasta for Jessica. Lauren and Jessica talked about their grandchildren while Emma picked at her salad.

"You look like someone spat in your salad," Lauren said, and it took Emma a moment to realize Lauren was talking to her.

"What? Oh, no, just thinking," Emma answered.

"You've definitely got something on your mind. What's going on?" Jessica asked.

Emma paused, searching for the words to explain the sudden wave of insecurity that had washed over her as they sat at lunch.

"It's just, I don't think I'll ever be able to do that," she said.

"Do what?" Lauren sat back against the booth and wiped her face with her napkin.

"What you two did. You noticed the dancers weren't comfortable, and you figured out how to get them to open up." Emma shook her head and moved a tomato around her plate with her fork. "I just don't think I'll ever have those instincts."

"Instinct?" Jessica said, and laughed. "Emma, we've been doing this independently for longer than you've been on this planet, and working together for the last fifteen years. What you're calling instinct is literally decades of practice."

"You can't expect to know everything about a job you've only been on for a week," Lauren added. "You should have seen the both of us when we started. I rewrote my first article so many times, I probably still could recite it for you word for word."

"Mine too!" Jessica exclaimed. "My first employer wasn't very forgiving, either. I was sure he was either going to fire me or send me back to the mailroom after the eighth time I gave him the same article."

"And that didn't bother you? All that rejection?" Emma asked. She had dealt with criticisms on her college papers, but she had always justified that it was just classwork. When Blake had criticized her poem, it had felt like he had cut off a piece of her soul.

"Of course it bothered me, failure isn't fun for anybody. But what was the alternative, give up?"

Emma shrugged.

"Listen Emma," Jessica said, leaning forward. "You're going to get criticisms, but you will learn from those. You're going to write a bad article that you might have to rewrite a thousand times, but something new will happen with each rewrite. You will have bad days, bad interviews, bad analogies, bad grammar. But listen to me – you will get better. I can tell how much you want to do this, and that drive will carry you through all those bad things. Embrace failure. Failing at something you want to do is a much better option than just not doing it."

"I guess," she replied.

Emma went back to her salad as her two colleagues returned to the subject of grandchildren.

Embrace failure.

The thought of failing at this job terrified Emma. What if she had moved a thousand miles just to get fired? Would that destroy her dream completely? The 'what ifs' scared Emma, but what was the alternative? She could have stayed in San Diego and continued working at a stable, risk-free job that she hated. Was that a better decision than the possibility that she might fail at something she might actually love?

And if Jessica was right, if Emma did learn how to be a successful writer, wouldn't that be worth everything Emma had already given up, and what she might experience in the future?

With all of the questions running through her mind, Emma knew she'd have plenty for her journal that evening.

CHAPTER 19

Emma spent the rest of the week balancing her time at the coffee shop with her days at the magazine where she continued working with Jessica on the dance competition article, and learning the process of editing and release of an article. She'd waited a few days to respond to Blake, considering just ignoring him altogether, but didn't want to lose her deposit and finally replied. After waiting another day, she realized that he wasn't going to respond further.

She hadn't spent any real time with Jason since their chat on the river, which she felt both relieved and anxious about. One the one hand, not spending time with someone who was clearly caring and interesting was a potential negative. On the other hand, not spending time with Jason meant that she wouldn't be tempted to ignore her 'not ready to date' mentality, since she felt attracted both to his personality and his looks. Throughout the week, she'd tried to convince herself that he was likely more flawed than she imagined, that his kindness to her at the river was just a fluke. She'd managed to convince herself believing that all the way through the end of her Friday shift, when she packed her things and ran into Jason on her way out, waiting for the elevator.

Again.

She reminded herself again that it was time to start that resolution to take the stairs.

"How was your second week, Emma? I haven't seen you since last Saturday," Jason said, smiling at her.

Asking about her day wasn't exactly a flaw, Emma thought.

"Oh, it's been pretty busy. I'm done with training at the coffee shop, and it's almost non-stop customers. And in here, I've been trying to keep up with Jessica and Lauren all week."

"Those two are a handful," he said, laughing. "Really productive as a team. They've been joined at the hip since before I started here. I don't know what Lauren is going to do when Jessica leaves."

"Yeah, I don't know how I'm ever going to learn everything I can from her before she's gone."

The elevator dinged and the doors slid open slowly. Again, Jason held his arm out to allow Emma to go in before following her.

Consistently exhibiting gentlemanly behavior was also definitely not a flaw.

"I've been working here over ten years, and I still haven't learned everything I can. It's a constant process."

Emma nodded, but still wasn't convinced.

"What are your plans for the weekend?" Jason said, and Emma blinked at the change of subject.

"Um, nothing yet," she said.

"Great," Jason said, his smile widening. "It's my brother's birthday, and I'm having a barbeque at my place tomorrow afternoon. I'd love for you to come, if you're free."

Emma paused as they reached the ground floor and the elevator doors opened. Once again, Jason somehow managed to open the door to the building for her, despite letting her out of the elevator first. She marveled at his insistence to be a gentleman while she tried to come up with a reason why she couldn't go.

"It won't be too big a party, just a handful of friends," Jason continued. "I just thought, since you're new in town, you might like to get to know some people."

"Yeah, definitely," she said, agreeing to the fact that she was new in town. When Jason smiled bigger, she realized her miscommunication, but it was too late.

"Great," Jason said, then pulled out his phone. "What's your phone number? I'll text you my address."

"Okay," Emma stammered, and rattled off her number.

Friends, friends, friends, she repeated to herself in her mind. He's just inviting you because you're new in town and he's being friendly.

Emma watched him type her phone number into his phone and noticed that his fingernails were short, and she found herself wondering if he clipped them short or bit them off absent-mindedly. Thinking of him biting his nails made Emma think about his mouth, and she wondered if it tasted as good as the rest of him smelled.

Friends! her brain shouted, and Emma nearly smacked herself in the forehead.

"Okay, sent," Jason said, and Emma felt her phone buzz in her purse.

"Should I bring anything?" Emma asked, but Jason shook his head.

"I think we have plenty of food and drinks, so just bring yourself. Oh, and Marcy will probably be there, in case you need a ride."

"I'll talk to her, thanks," Emma said.

"Okay great," Jason said, then turned towards his truck at the far end of the parking lot. He smiled, then waved as Emma climbed into her car and started the engine.

"Friends," she said aloud, then bit down on her lip as she watched Jason's jeans shift against his ass as he walked to his truck.

"One more time, with feeling," she said, then pulled out of her parking space and headed home, saying the word 'friends' twenty times before she hit the highway.

CHAPTER 20

The next afternoon, Emma found herself in a conversation with another of Jason's brothers, who was just as tall and even more muscular. John, the birthday boy, was a microbiologist, and traveled around the country taking water samples of various lakes and rivers. After seeing how gorgeous Jason and his brothers were, Emma herself was wondering what was in the water.

"So, how do you like Montana so far?" John asked.

"It's beautiful," Emma answered. "And the people are really friendly. I didn't know any of my neighbors back in San Diego, but the woman across the street came over the first morning I was here, and almost every day since."

"Some of that is just Maxine," John said with a laugh. "She's friendly, sure, but there's a hunger for gossip in there as well."

"How'd you know Maxine was my neighbor?" Emma asked.

"She mentioned it," John said. "We have family dinners on Sunday nights. Maxine and my grandmother have been friends forever, so she comes every once in a while. She came by the week before you moved in. You should've seen her, she was more excited than I've seen her in years."

"Well I'm glad to hear it," Emma said. "Although the novelty must have worn off. I haven't seen her for almost a week."

"What'd you do?" John asked.

"What do you mean?"

"You've been here, what, two weeks? There's no way Maxine already knows your entire life story, and even if she did, she'd still come over. So you must've done something."

"I swear, I didn't do anything," Emma protested.

"Do anything to who?"

The hair on Emma's arms stood up as she heard Jason's voice, and smelled his familiar musky scent. She looked up into his smiling green eyes, and couldn't help but smile back.

"Maxine," she answered. "Your brother thinks I did something to upset her."

"I'm sure you didn't," Jason said.

"Tell him why," John countered, and Emma furrowed her brows at him.

"She came by every other day the first week I was here, but I haven't seen her at all this past week."

"Wow," Jason said. "What did you do?"

"Nothing!" Emma protested again, and John laughed.

As Emma continued to defend herself, Marcy walked over, dreamy-eyed, with Jason's brother Jeff.

"Good to see you again, Emma," Jeff said, shaking her hand. "We're about to go to the backyard and play some shuffleboard. Stacy is already playing, so we need a fourth, if you don't mind us stealing Jason away."

"How about I step in," John interjected. "I think Jason was about to give Emma the grand tour."

"Works for me," Jeff said.

Emma thought she noticed a look between John and his younger brother, but was distracted by Jeff's hand on Marcy's lower back as he led her to the backyard.

Jason cleared his throat, and looked down at Emma.

"You don't actually have to go on a tour of the house," he said.

"No, I'd love to," Emma answered. She wanted to see his house, wanted to spend time with him, but seeing him in his element, with his family, was doing nothing to quell her growing crush. He was friendly, kind, and welcoming to everyone at the party. She tried to remind herself that drooling all over his carpet would do nothing to further their friendship, so she just held her arm out.

"Lead the way."

"Well, you've already seen the kitchen and living room," he said.

"I have, and it's beautiful," Emma said.

The kitchen was larger than Emma's, with new appliances and a small table in a nook next to a window in the corner. Jason's house wasn't a log cabin, but he'd left exposed wood beams overhead that gave it an open, outdoor feeling.

The kitchen and living room were one large, connected room. The front door of the house led directly into the living room, and the entire front of the A-frame house was windows. Emma could imagine that on a clear night, Jason could sit on his couch and stare straight out to the stars.

A hallway led from the kitchen past a small bedroom that looked to double as an office, and a bathroom before leading out to the backyard.

As Jason led Emma upstairs, she marveled at the photography that lined every wall.

"These are all yours?" she asked.

"They are," he answered.

"They're incredible," she said. She passed scenes of snow-lined creeks, granite mountains rising out of the fog, desert sunsets.

"What made you decide to build your own house?" Emma asked as they reached the landing at the top of the stairs.

"Well, originally I was planning just to buy a house. But I kept looking, and I just wasn't seeing what I wanted. I had an image in my head, and I just couldn't find it. Once I got that image in my head, buying anything else felt like settling. So I drew up what I wanted, and worked with an architect and an engineer to figure out all of the specifics."

Jason opened a door into the bedroom that took up the entire second floor, which was like an oversized loft. Again, one wall was made almost entirely of windows, and Emma looked out onto Jason's backyard where the rest of his guests were below.

Beyond the backyard, Emma saw nothing but acre upon acre of tall trees.

"And you did this all yourself?" she asked.

"I had help," Jason answered, joining her at the window. "Having three brothers comes with its advantages."

"I can only imagine."

Emma felt Jason's arm brush against hers and she looked up at him, surprised to find him watching her. He wasn't quite smiling, but the way he was looking at her made Emma swallow hard.

"I could use a beer," she said, and Jason smiled.

"Of course. Lead the way," he said.

Back outside, Jason led Emma to a bench swing hanging from a large tree branch. As they walked, grasshoppers popped up from the grass in front of them like bacon grease in a hot pan. The swing was close enough to the party that Emma could watch Marcy flirt with Jeff, but far enough that she and Jason could hear each other.

They sat together, swinging in silence, while the party happened in front of them. The night was warm enough that Emma didn't need a sweater, but the occasional breeze would push through the trees and remind her a change of seasons might be on its way. Seasons didn't really exist in San Diego. It was either warm and cloudy, or warm and sunny. It never really got cold, the weather was always just different degrees of warm.

"Writing the next great novel in your head?" Jason teased, and Emma realized how long she'd been sitting with him, not talking.

"No." She smiled. "Just thinking about how different it is here than in San Diego."

"Do you miss it?" Jason asked.

"I've been wondering about that," Emma replied.

She had been writing in her journal every night, mainly about her new house and job, occasionally about Blake. But even though she'd only been in Montana a couple of weeks, she found that each day, she was writing more about her new life and less about what she'd left behind.

"I don't know that I miss it," she said finally. "I think I expected to, so it's more that I'm feeling surprised at how little I do miss."

"Do you have family down there?"

"No," Emma said, shaking her head. "My mom lives on the east coast with her husband and their kids."

"Are you close with your parents?"

"Not exactly," Emma said, sighing.

"I'm sorry if I've over-stepped. You don't have to talk about it if you don't want to."

"No, it's fine," Emma said, waving her hand. "It's just sort of a long story."

Jason sat back in the swing and smiled. "I've got nothing but time."

Emma took a deep breath and looked out onto the field that comprised Jason's enormous back yard.

"My parents had me when they were really young. Teenagers. My mom did the best she could, I think, but I always felt a little like the water that squeezes out of the ketchup bottle if you don't shake it up enough."

Emma looked back at Jason, who was frowning.

"I'm not sure I understand."

"It's like when you want ketchup on your food, but you squeeze the bottle and the first thing that comes out is this watery mess that you have to just deal with until what you really want comes out," Emma said, then shrugged. "Like I said, my mom did her best with me. I spent a lot of time with my grandparents until they passed away when I was in high school. My mom started dating her husband right when I started college, and we grew apart pretty quickly. They got married and moved across the country, and then she had two kids with him. I guess I always felt like she was giving herself a second chance at the life she really wanted. I was just an accident that happened when she forgot to shake the bottle."

"I'm sorry, Emma," Jason said, and Emma shook her head.

"It's okay. I don't blame her, really. She was a kid when she had me, and once I was old enough to take care of myself, she went after what she needed. I think it hurt me for a while, but I can't really hold onto it anymore. We email occasionally, she's happy."

"How about your dad?" Jason asked.

Emma stared at the sky, pushing her toes against the ground in time with Jason's gentle swinging.

"My dad..." she said, trailing off.

"If that's too personal-" Jason started, but Emma waved him off.

"It's not," she said, even though she hadn't talked about her dad with more than a handful of people her entire life. Something about being with Jason on a porch swing under a giant blue sky brought her guard down.

"My dad was just distant, I guess. It never really felt like he liked me all that much. It was inconsistent, but I spent weekends with him sometimes when I was young. I was always just trying so hard to get him to want me around, to be interested in what I was doing. Finally, when I was in high school, he kept having all these reasons why I couldn't come over, so we just talked on the phone a few times a month."

"I'm sorry," Jason said. "Do you talk to him now?"

Emma shook her head.

"Not really. Sometimes I'll call on holidays, or he'll call me. But if my mom wasn't ready for me, my dad was even less ready. He still doesn't have kids, so I don't think he ever really wanted to be a father. He just had to fake it. Turns out he wasn't that good of an actor."

"So you haven't seen him since you were a teenager?" Jason asked.

"Just once," Emma answered. "At my college graduation."

And suddenly, she was back there. She had been in a sea of students and their families, and her mom and her mom's new husband had walked up to congratulate Emma.

Marcy's family had been standing nearby, and Marcy had hugged Emma's mother and congratulated her.

Emma had looked up and her father was ten yards away. She'd walked up to him and he'd given her an awkward hug.

"Congratulations," he'd said.

Emma had thanked him. During college, Emma accepted that her dad might not have been the kind of father she wanted, and maybe that was okay. But there he had been, at her graduation, so that must have meant something.

"What's that?" he had asked her, gesturing to the journal, and Emma had told him.

He had squinted at her, and his mouth had twisted up.

"A degree in writing? I didn't even know they made those. Sounds like a waste of paper. What are you gonna do with that?"

"I want to be a writer," she'd told him.

He'd scratched the back of his neck, and shook his head.

Every detail remained burned into Emma's mind so many years later, as though it were happening in front of her.

"He said, he didn't know why my mom had filled my head with such bullshit. I should have gotten a real degree where I could make money, instead of just spending a lot of money to be a cashier at a grocery store."

Emma's voice hitched as she told Jason the story. It was that comment that had first put the darkness of doubt in her head, when the fire of her dreams first started turning to ash.

"Emma, I'm so sorry," Jason said, and put his hand on her shoulder. "I shouldn't have been so pushy."

"No, really, it's okay," Emma said, straightening her back. "You do have a strange way of getting me to tell you things I shouldn't though," she added.

"It's a gift," he said with a wink.

"I know mostly he was just trying to criticize my mom for encouraging me when I was young, which was one of the things that I will always appreciate her for, even if we aren't close now. But it came out as a slight against me. I still think about what he said. I know I take responsibility for my own life, my own decisions, but those words crept into my mind every time I thought about writing or quitting my old job."

"Our parents have more power over us than we like to admit, I think," Jason said.

They sat in silence a while longer, and Emma felt her anger and sadness fade away with each creak of the swing.

"It really is a big sky," Emma said, staring up at the bright blue that stretched from one horizon to another.

"I've tried so many times to capture it in a photograph, but I don't think I ever get it completely right. There's a feeling I get when I look up at it, the vastness, that I just can't translate into a photo."

"Hope," Emma said, and Jason nodded at her before looking back to the sky.

"That's it," he said.

They watched the shuffleboard game progress, and by the high-fiving, it looked as though Marcy and Jeff were in the lead.

"Your turn," Emma said, and Jason turned to her and tilted his head. "You got me to open up to you. Our friendship deal is that we're equal, so it's your turn."

Jason laughed, nodding. "How about this – I'll help you figure out why Maxine is mad at you."

"She isn't mad at me!" Emma protested.

"You haven't seen her for a week?"

"I've seen her walking around her property, but she hasn't come over, no."

"What happened the last time you saw her?" Jason asked.

Emma sighed and closed her eyes.

"She came over to have tea and watch me with the cats," Emma started.

"Cats?"

"The ones from under the porch," Emma said, opening her eyes to frown at Jason, and he mimed zipping his mouth shut.

Concentrating, Emma closed her eyes again.

"We talked, she finished her tea, then I gave her a dish back and she went home."

"What dish?"

"Oh, she made me some meat casserole thing the day I got here, so I gave the dish back," Emma answered.

"What was in the dish?"

"Nothing," Emma said, "I cleaned it. You think I'd give her back a dirty dish?"

"That's what you did," Jason said, pointing his finger at Emma.

Emma frowned.

"I am so confused."

"Maxine is a very particular woman," Jason said, then took a sip of beer from his cup. "If she brought over food, you're supposed to make food in the same dish as a 'thank you' before you give it back."

"How was I supposed to know that?" Emma asked, both concerned that she'd offended Maxine and frustrated that her mother had never taught her the 'rules' to being neighborly.

"It's okay, just go over there and make amends. She's stubborn, but Maxine doesn't hold a grudge long. As long as the other person gives in first, of course."

"Of course," Emma groaned. "Your brother said you have Maxine over for family dinners?"

Jason nodded. "Not every Sunday, but at least once a month. She doesn't have much family left, but since she and my grandma have been friends for so long, Maxine is almost like a second grandma."

"Oh great," Emma said. "So I should probably watch what I tell her so your whole family doesn't know my life story?"

"She seems like a gossip, but she's more curious than anything. She won't say anything about you that you wouldn't tell us yourself," Jason said, and Emma felt more at ease. She hadn't told Maxine anything much already, but it was only a matter of time.

From across the yard, Emma heard Marcy yelp and throw her hands in the air. She high-fived Jeff before jumping into his large arms for a hug.

"Hey younger brother, come see if you can challenge the champions!" Jeff called, then set Marcy down on the grass.

"You up for it?" Jason asked, and Emma almost declined. She'd never played shuffleboard, and was afraid she would be terrible. But Lauren and Jessica's motto crept to her head, and she changed her mind.

Embrace failure, she told herself, then nodded to Jason and stood up.

"Maxine told me something about you," she teased as they walked towards the group, feeling bold after managing a whole conversation with Jason without drooling.

"What's that?" Jason asked.

"She said you're sex on a stick," Emma answered, trying to hold back her laughter as she heard Jason spit out his beer behind her.

After the barbeque, Emma dropped a tipsy Marcy back at her house in town, then drove back to the cabin. Maxine's porch light was still on when Emma drove by, as she usually didn't turn it off until after ten every night. Emma pulled into her dirt driveway and parked, then marched to Maxine's house and knocked on the front door. It opened right away, which meant Maxine was probably waiting by the door when Emma knocked.

"Yes?" Maxine's always-penetrating eyes were laced with a hint of curiosity, and somehow she still managed to be intimidating in a flower-print bathrobe.

"I need your dish back," Emma huffed, out of breath after her quick trek across the street.

"My dish? I'm sure the cabin has plenty of kitchenware," she answered.

"I have plenty, but I need yours back. I did it wrong."

"I know it's been a while since I've been to California, but I don't remember it being a state of crazy people," Maxine said, folding her arms.

"Maxine, work with me here. Just bring me the dish."

The old woman paused before shuffling into her kitchen. Emma considered following, but realized she hadn't been invited inside, and didn't want to add another grievance to Maxine's growing tally. She waited outside and listened to clinking and drawers opening until Maxine finally reappeared at the door with the empty dish in her hand.

"Thank you," Emma said, taking the dish and turning from the door. She headed down the steps and made it halfway to the street before she turned around.

"Dinner is at six tomorrow night," she called to Maxine. "Don't be late!"

Emma couldn't be sure in the dancing shadows of the porch light, but she thought she saw the old woman smile before she shut the door.

CHAPTER 21

The following evening, Maxine leaned back in her chair on the porch and sipped her tea while Emma sat on the steps, the kittens clambering back and forth across her lap and under the porch. Marcy was inside washing dishes and packaging leftovers, despite Emma's insistence that she leave it. Emma had invited Marcy over for backup in case Maxine was still giving her the silent treatment, just so she'd have someone to talk to during dinner. But as soon as Maxine saw her dish on the kitchen table filled with a lasagna Emma had spent all day making, all seemed to be forgiven and they had a nice dinner. And it was fortunate that Marcy had come along, as they spent more time talking about her growing relationship with Jeff than Emma's interactions with Jason.

The phone rang inside as Marcy was cleaning, and Emma heard her answer it.

"One second. Who can I say is calling?"

Emma heard a pause as Marcy stepped to the front door and held out the phone, a strange look on her face.

"Who is it?" Emma asked as she stood to take the phone.

Marcy waited a moment before mouthing, "Blake."

Emma was so surprised she nearly dropped the phone, but managed to hold on and raise it to her ear as she walked into the cabin and shut Marcy and Maxine outside.

"Hello?"

"Emma, hi. I tried your cellphone but it just kept going to voicemail. Liz gave me this number."

Emma frowned and reminded herself to send Liz a strongly-worded email when she got off the phone.

"Yeah, I don't get great service out at the cabin."

"No service? I didn't know that was even possible."

"Well, Blake, it is," Emma said, wondering if the reason for his call was to point out the many failings of the cell phone carrier service business.

"And a cabin? That sounds quaint."

Emma bit her lip and said nothing. Blake had only ever used the word 'quaint' once, when they had rented a room at a bed and breakfast in Northern California. Emma had loved the rustic nature of the place, but Blake had seemed to use 'quaint' when he couldn't think of a nice way to say 'old, dirty, and cheap'.

"So, how are you? How is it out there in Montana?"

"Good. The job's going okay, the cabin's really nice and the rent is reasonable, and it's just beautiful out here with all the trees and open space."

Emma felt defensive, suspicious as to why he called after only one text message in weeks. He also said 'Montana' as though she had moved to outer space rather than just a few states away.

"Well, that sounds just great."

"It is," Emma agreed.

When she moved to Montana, all she had wanted was for Blake to wonder about her, ask about her. She had imagined all the ways she would make him feel guilty for leaving her. Now that she had him on the phone, she just felt confused.

"Was there something that you wanted?" she asked.

"Yeah," he said, then paused for so long that Emma wondered if they'd lost their connection.

"I'm seeing someone."

Emma had thought of a few things Blake was calling to tell her, maybe that he missed her, maybe that he had found something of hers when he was moving out, maybe that he needed a kidney and was wondering if she had a spare. A new relationship wasn't one of the bits of information she expected.

"Emma?" he asked, when she hadn't said anything.

"I'm here," she said.

"I know it's a surprise, but I just wanted to let you know personally, before anyone else did or you saw it online."

"Okay," she said.

"Well, I don't want to keep you too long, so I'll let you go," Blake said.

Emma checked the clock over the microwave and noticed they'd been on the phone for less than three minutes.

"Sure thing."

She thought about adding a 'thanks for calling' or 'I appreciate the heads up', but neither felt true. She'd spent the last month distancing herself from Blake, getting over him, and his call did nothing to further either of those goals.

"Enjoy Montana," he said, again saying the word as if it were a mystical land. "I'm sure if you gave your old boss a call, he could rescue you from that cabin and bring you back to a world where cell phones exist," he added, then laughed.

"Cell phones exist here, Blake," she yelled into the phone, but he was already gone.

She stared at the phone for another minute, annoyed, but she couldn't pinpoint what was bothering her the most.

Emma hung up the phone and walked outside, then plopped onto the porch and pulled a kitten into her lap. They'd been playing so long that he didn't struggle, and she stroked his soft fur and watched as he closed his eyes and began to fall asleep.

"Everything okay?" Marcy asked, and Emma sighed.

"It's fine," Emma lied.

"It doesn't look fine," Maxine said. "What happened?"

"Apparently Blake has a new girlfriend," Emma said.

Marcy and Maxine stared at Emma. Marcy looked confused, and Maxine looked pissed.

"Why the hell would he call to tell you that?" Maxine demanded.

"He said he wanted to let me know first, before anyone else told me," Emma said with a shrug. "I think he was trying to be nice."

"Bullshit," Maxine spurted, and Marcy raised her eyebrows. "Nice people don't call their ex-girlfriends to let them know they've moved on. He was calling to gloat."

Marcy nodded while Emma thought it over. While she still had enough good memories of Blake to believe that he wasn't a complete jerk, she knew Maxine had a point.

"I guess you could be right," she conceded.

"Of course I am," Maxine said, leaning back in her chair.

"Did he say anything else?" Marcy asked.

"Just that if I called my old boss, he could probably 'rescue me' and bring me back to San Diego."

"Rescue you?" Maxine and Marcy said in unison. Marcy laughed, but Maxine looked angry all over again.

"It seems like you rescued yourself from a bad job and a bad situation, not the other way around," Maxine said. "What did you tell him?"

"Nothing," Emma said, shrugging.

"Nothing?"

"What was I supposed to say? That Montana is beautiful, that I've made more friends here in two weeks than in my last two years in San Diego? That I hated my old job, and my new life is difficult but could potentially make me very happy? That he's an asshole and I can't believe how much time I'd wasted on him? That him dumping me was probably the best thing that could've happened?"

"For starters," Maxine said.

"What's the point? I was never good enough while we were dating, apparently. And trying to compete with him now would just make me feel like I'm trying to justify myself for decisions he will never understand. He'll think that I still want him to accept me. To love me."

The three women were quiet for a few minutes, enjoying the soft snores of the sleeping kittens and the rhythmic thumping of a woodpecker against a tree in the yard.

"Love is important," Maxine said, breaking the silence and sipping her tea as she stared through the trees into the setting sun. "But love from someone else isn't the only kind you need to be looking for. More than anything, you need to be able to love yourself. If you can't do that, nothing else you find will fill that void."

They again sat in silence until the sun dipped below the horizon and the air turned cold, and they said their goodbyes before Marcy walked Maxine back to her house with her dish filled with leftover lasagna.

Emma went inside and watched the stars begin to shine against the darkening sky from her kitchen window, wondering how she went nearly thirty years without knowing how many of them were out there. She had just needed to find the right perspective to see them.

She thought about herself. How long she'd spent living a life she didn't enjoy, just because she didn't really know what she was capable of. But here in the woods, in a small cabin surrounded by trees, cats, and a nosy neighbor, Emma was beginning to realize that there might be much more to her than she'd always led herself to believe. She'd just needed a shift in perspective.

Emma looked at the phone hanging on the wall, then back out to the brilliant night sky.

"I don't need to be rescued," she told the stars confidently, and sat on her bed to write that mantra over and over between the details of her weekend.

CHAPTER 22

"I don't need to be rescued. I do NOT need to be rescued," Emma muttered to herself, hoping the repetition might make it true. But as she stared out at the line of customers in front of the cash register, as well as the small group next to the pick-up counter growing impatient as they waited for their drinks, Emma felt much less sure of herself.

It was a Friday afternoon, less than a week after her call with Blake. Between the internship and coffee schedule, Emma found she had almost no time to think about him, and realized that when she did, the anger she had been holding for him was beginning to dissipate. And after three weeks of her new schedule, Emma was beginning to believe she'd gotten a handle on it.

As though the universe wanted to prove her wrong, the college student who was supposed to work the Friday afternoon shift with her never showed up. Emma had called Mike, who'd promised to call in someone to take the shift, but the replacement hadn't shown up yet. In a twist of fate, that Friday was the busiest Emma had seen since she'd started at the coffee shop. Or maybe it just seemed that way since she was there alone.

"Okay Emma, you can do this," she told herself.

To the person waiting at the register, she said, "I apologize for the wait. Just give me a moment to get these orders and I'll be right with you."

Emma checked the receipts lining the counter in front of her, then started on two hot chocolates and two lattes while she heated up a muffin in the toaster oven. Emma loved Mike's coffee and treats, and preparing each cup to order was clearly the industry standard, but in that moment she found herself wishing he just made one giant vat of coffee and a batch of cold muffins she could hand out to everyone.

As those orders were almost ready, Emma took the order of the next two people at the counter. By the time she was done, the muffin was ready to serve with the lattes, and she gave them to the waiting customers before preparing the orders she'd just taken.

Within ten minutes, Emma had managed to take orders from the ten people who'd been waiting in line, and just two were left waiting for their order. As she poured the last two coffees into their respective cups, she saw someone out of the corner of her eye approach the register.

"Just one moment and I'll be right with you," Emma said, then propelled herself to the pick-up counter.

"Again, I'm so sorry for the wait. Please come back soon," she said, handing the customers their drinks before they turned and head out the door.

Emma took a deep breath and rolled her head around on her neck before approaching the register. She stopped when she saw the face on the other side of the counter smiling at her.

"Jason, hi," she said. "I'm sorry, I didn't notice it was you before."

"I don't blame you. It's been pretty crazy in here the last few minutes."

"You saw that?" Emma asked, hoping she hadn't looked as frazzled as she felt.

"I figured I'd wait for the line to die down before adding to your load. Is it usually just you here?"

"No, there are at least two of us, but my shift partner was a no-show, and the replacement Mike called hasn't come in yet."

"Well, I think you did pretty well on your own," Jason said. "I think you must've set a land speed record for coffee delivery."

"It didn't feel that way with the impatient stares I was rightfully getting, but thanks," Emma said. "Anyway, can I get you anything?"

"Right," Jason said, then looked up at the menu behind Emma.

As he looked, the door opened, and Mike breezed in through the door.

"Emma, I am so sorry. I'd called Julia to come in, but I guess she got caught up and will be another twenty minutes. I'll be here to help you until then."

Mike pulled an apron over his clothes as he walked behind the counter to join Emma.

"Tom has been a no-show once before, and got a warning. I was sure he wouldn't do it again, but I guess that will be his last chance. Again, I apologize. How'd everything go here on your own?"

"Okay I guess," Emma said with a shrug.

"She was amazing," Jason said from across the counter, and Emma looked back to see him staring at her, again with that face she didn't quite understand. It was almost a smile, but mostly it looked like he was trying to tell her something with his eyes, and she just couldn't interpret it.

"Thanks," Emma said, blushing. "Did you decide what you wanted?"

Jason stared at her for another few seconds, and Emma found her face growing hot under his gaze.

"I'll have the medium roast, black," he said finally, still staring at Emma.

"What size, Jason?" Mike asked. "I'll get that started while she finishes ringing you up and we'll have you out of here in no time."

"Biggest cup you've got," Jason said, then reached back to pull out his wallet as Mike got started on the order.

"Thanks for that," Emma said once Mike was out of earshot. "You didn't have to, but it's always nice for the boss to hear good things."

"Just the truth," Jason said, shrugging as he handed Emma his credit card. She rang him up and returned the card and receipt.

"So, what are you up to tonight?" Emma asked as Jason remained by the cash register. There were still customers at tables, but no one else in line.

"Running a few errands at the moment, then I've got some editing to do on a few freelance projects I've been working on. Then probably just read and go to bed."

"Not going out dancing tonight?" Emma asked, and Jason smiled.

"Not without my favorite dance partner," Jason answered, and Emma blushed.

"We'll have to go again sometime. It's always good to have a friend other than Marcy and Maxine to hang out with," she added.

"Here's your coffee," Mike said, handing the cup across the counter. "Hey, how's your family? I played basketball with his brother, Jeff, in high school," he added.

Finally, Jason looked away from Emma, but his expression had altered. The half-smile was gone, and his eyes had changed, but she couldn't put her finger on how it looked different.

"They're just fine, thanks."

"From what I hear, Marcy has been spending a lot of time with Jeff lately," Mike said, and Jason laughed.

"I think you'd have to ask Marcy about that."

"Fair enough," Mike answered. "Emma, I'm going to run into the back for a minute. Do you have everything covered up here?"

"Yep," Emma answered with a nod. Despite the customers chatting quietly as they sipped their drinks, Emma felt alone with Jason.

"Was there something else?" Emma asked as he lingered in front of the counter.

Jason opened his mouth, but closed it as the door opened and an older woman walked in.

"Jason, here you are," the woman said as she approached. "I thought you'd be done already."

The woman glanced at Emma and smiled before turning back to Jason, tucking her thick, grey hair behind her ears. She wore a long maroon coat over jeans and a blouse, and looked to be wearing a pair of boots almost identical to the ones Marcy had purchased for Emma on her first night out in Montana.

"Sorry, mom. Just catching up with Emma here," Jason said, nodding in Emma's direction.

Jason's mother turned to Emma and her smile widened as she stepped closer to the counter.

"Oh Emma, I've heard so much about you. Between Maxine and Jason, I feel like I already know you."

Emma glanced at Jason, but he just smiled before putting his coffee cup to his lips.

"Hopefully good things," Emma said.

"Of course. I'm Cathy," she said, reaching her hand across the counter. Emma wiped her hands on her apron before taking Cathy's hand.

"How are you liking Missoula so far?"

"I love it," Emma answered. "There's so much open space, and everyone has been so friendly. I am a little nervous about driving once the snow hits, but other than that, I'm enjoying myself."

"Driving in the snow is just like anything, a little practice and you'll get right used to it," Cathy said. "And how do you like living out at the cabin? I've always loved that neighborhood."

"It's fantastic. I can't believe how quiet it is. I've shared a wall with multiple people for the last few years, so it's a little strange not to have neighbors right on top of each other. Although Maxine isn't exactly shy about coming over," Emma added, and Cathy laughed.

"Maxine is a lot of things, but shy has definitely never been one of them," Cathy agreed, then turned to Jason. "Speaking of Maxine, she was planning to come over for Sunday dinner this weekend, wasn't she?"

"I think so," Jason nodded. "John or I was planning to go pick her up."

"Emma, would you join us? If you don't already have plans, of course."

Emma paused and looked at Jason, trying to judge how he felt. He just smiled and took another sip of his coffee.

"That would be great, if I wouldn't be imposing," she said.

Cathy waved her hand. "Not at all, the more the merrier. In fact, I think Marcy might be coming as well, so it'll be a great big group. We usually start early, so Jason can come pick you and Maxine up around three thirty?"

"Don't be silly, I can drive Maxine and myself over there."

"Are you sure? I don't want you to feel we're using you as her chauffer."

"Not at all," Emma said. "Can I bring anything?" she added. She'd already gotten into trouble by neglecting to bring Maxine a dish; she didn't want to offend Jason's entire family.

"You're already bringing yourself and Maxine, and we always have more than enough food. Jason, do you have her phone number so that you can call in case anything changes?"

"I do," Jason answered.

"Wonderful," Cathy said. "I just have one more errand I need to run, Jason, then I'll drop you off at home. He's such a good son, running around town to do my errands with me. His father has always hated shopping."

"Just an excuse to spend time with you, mom," Jason said, and Cathy put her arm around him.

"See what I mean? Anyway, it was lovely to meet you, Emma. We'll see you Sunday."

"Sounds good," Emma answered as Cathy turned towards the door.

"See you Sunday, Emma," Jason echoed. "And thanks for the coffee," he said, raising his cup. He turned and followed his mother, then waved again before stepping outside.

Emma took a deep breath and let it out before washing her hands. She thought about dinner with Jason and his family, and tried to remind herself that it wasn't anything to be nervous about. It was just an evening with her new friend and his family, some of whom she'd already met. Marcy would be there, and so would Maxine.

Maxine. Emma would have to tell her that she'd have a new driver for Sunday dinner at Jason's house.

O'SHEA

Something told her that Maxine already knew.

CHAPTER 23

"Emma, so nice to finally meet you. I'm Justin."

Emma looked up at the behemoth of a man who she would've known was a brother of Jason's even if he hadn't told her. He had the same hair color and dimple in his cheek, and seemed to have grown up on the same water source that made his three brothers look like they walked straight out of a super hero comic book.

"Nice to meet you Justin," Emma said, shaking his hand.

"And this is my wife, Regina," he added as he put his arm around the waist of the woman beside him. Her hair was long and blonde, and her blue eyes were as bright as any lake Emma had ever seen.

"Emma, good to meet you," Regina said, shaking Emma's hand.

"You too. Maxine told me you have twin girls?"

"And one on the way," Regina said, rubbing her stomach. "Just another three months. I was sure that we'd have all boys because of Justin's family, but now we need to find another girl name."

Justin looked down at his wife and kissed the top of her head, smiling before he put his own hand on her stomach.

"I'm the luckiest man alive," he said, and Regina smiled up at him. "Speaking of, where are the girls?"

"They're out with your dad in the barn, I think."

They stood in the living room of Jason's parents' home surrounded by photos of all four boys from the time they were babies until recently. Emma thought she spotted a photo of Jason at a high school dance with bleached blonde spiked hair, and she reminded herself to take a closer look as soon as she got a chance.

"Hey Emma, Marcy told me you'd be here."

Marcy and Jeff approached from the entry room, holding hands, and Emma hugged Marcy as she got close enough.

"Yep, I couldn't turn down the offer of a home cooked meal. And a chance to see these amazing childhood photos of Jason," she said as Jason came out from the kitchen.

"There's a reason I decided to become the person behind the camera," he said. "Less chance that I could embarrass myself."

Jason's mother poked her head into the living room from the swinging kitchen door.

"Five minutes, everyone. Marcy, Jeff, could you help me set the table please?"

"Sure thing," Marcy answered.

"Can I do anything to help?" Emma asked.

"Yes, could someone go get the girls and my husband? They're outside somewhere. Oh never mind, here they come," she said, and Emma turned to see two teen girls and Jason's father approach the sliding glass door. Even through the door, Emma could see that they definitely got their mother's hair.

"Uncle Jason!" they said in unison before running up to him for a hug.

"Good to see you, girls. I have a friend I'd like you to meet."

The girls pulled away from their hug and turned to eye Emma. Something in their stare suddenly reminded her what it was like to be thirteen again, and she found herself wondering if she'd picked the right outfit.

"Hi, I'm Emma," she said. For a split second, Emma couldn't tell if they were going to ignore her or not the way she remembered being ignored at thirteen, but then one smiled, followed immediately by the other.

"Emma, oh my gosh, did you know that my grandpa has *bats* in the barn? They're super hard to get rid of," one of the girls said. She had her blonde hair in a braid and wore a long green dress with boots.

"Yeah, we keep telling him to get a barn cat to scare them off, but he won't," the other one said. Her hair was in a ponytail, and was wearing jeans and a sweater. Emma was thankful for the difference in their outfits, because other than the clothing, they were impossible to tell apart.

"Tell Emma your names before bombarding her with information," Regina said, shaking her head.

"Oh, I'm Mia," the girl in green said.

"And I'm Ally."

"And I'm Bill," Jason's father said, shaking Emma's hand. "Figured I'd get a word in while I could," he added with a wink.

"Cats would totally help, Grandpa," Mia said, and Ally nodded.

"You just want me to get cats so you can play with them when you're here," Bill said, raising his eyebrows.

"I have a few kittens at my house," Emma said, and tried not to laugh when the girls' eyes widened simultaneously. She wondered if they practiced their synchronicity, or if it was just a side effect of being a twin.

"You have *kittens*? More than one? How did you get them?"

"Where did they come from?"

"What color are they?"

"Please tell me you have pictures."

"Girls, slow down with the questions," Justin interjected, but Emma laughed.

"It's fine," she said. Before she could answer any of their questions, Cathy popped in from the dining room.

"Dinner is ready, come on in everyone," she announced.

"Emma, you *have* to sit next to us," Mia said.

"We're not supposed to look at our phones during dinner, but you can tell us about the kittens and we can look at their photos afterwards."

"That sounds good to me," Emma said, following them into the dining room.

Maxine and Jason's grandmother were already seated at the table, and Mia led Emma to a seat directly across from them, then she and her sister sat on either side of Emma.

"Cathy, this looks and smells amazing," Emma said, and Cathy nodded her head.

"Well, I'm just so glad you could join us," she responded, taking her seat near the head of the table. "Please don't be shy, everyone dig in."

Emma pulled her chair into the table and laid her napkin on her lap and piled a spoonful of potatoes onto her plate before passing to Ally beside her.

"Okay, so there are three kittens. And the mom?" Mia asked as she passed Emma the plate of vegetables.

"What about the dad?" Ally asked.

Emma had noticed that there was a rhythm to the girls' questions. Mia would start, and Ally would either provide a follow-up immediately, or nod to emphasize Mia's question. They were quite a tag-team.

"The mom is black, and I've convinced her to move indoors with her kittens. I haven't seen the male around anywhere."

"Aw, that's sad," Mia commented, and Ally nodded.

"It is, but they seem okay. I keep them pretty well-fed and entertained, although I'll admit that three kittens is quite a handful."

The girls exchanged a look, then nodded at each other and smiled. It seemed like another sibling or twin thing that Emma couldn't decipher, and she found, not for the first time, that she envied people with relationships so close. The closest thing Emma could compare to was Marcy, although Maxine was quickly becoming a frontrunner in the 'understanding Emma' department.

"Do you think she'll have any more kittens?" Mia asked, and Emma shook her head as she passed a plate of chicken to Ally.

"I'm taking them all to the vet to get shots, then to figure out when I can get them all fixed. I don't want any of them to get loose and have more kittens. With all the coyotes in my neighborhood, I'd hate for another litter to end up living under someone else's porch."

"That makes sense," Mia said, and Emma tried not to smile when she saw Ally nod in agreement. As she passed another plate in the endless train of food coming her way, Emma glanced up to see Jason watching her. She smiled, and he gave her another of his dimpled half-smiles before taking a plate from his grandmother.

Emma spent the next hour trying to concentrate on passing plates and eating while fielding questions from Mia and Ally. She thought they might slow down when they got food in their mouths, but their tag-team question strategy meant that while one was chewing, the other was talking. In terms of interview ability, they even gave Lauren and Jessica a run for their money. Emma decided at some point through the dinner that if she could learn to be half as comfortable asking questions as either one of them, she'd have no problem getting the job at the magazine.

She was also glad that they were both too young to apply.

CHAPTER 24

"Emma, thanks for coming in. Go ahead and shut the door."

Emma nodded, then shut Don's office door before sitting at the chair across from his desk. It was the Friday before Halloween, just over halfway through the internship, and Don had scheduled meetings with each intern. Emma was the last, and she felt her heart pounding as she sat in front of Don, despite his calming smile.

"The main purpose for us getting together is to review how you've been doing so far, and our goals for the rest of the year."

"Got it," Emma said, nodding again.

"First of all, how do you feel you're doing?"

"I think I'm learning a lot," Emma responded, sitting back in her chair. "Jessica and Lauren are incredibly helpful and patient, and they're showing me how to go from the research aspect of a story into something that people want to read."

Don nodded, then scribbled something on the notepad in front of him.

"And how do you think that transition is going?"

"The research is definitely what I'm more comfortable with, as opposed to the interview process."

"That is a skill, I agree, but Jessica and Lauren have mentioned you've made strides between the first article with the dance team and your visit with the theater group last week."

"I'm glad," Emma answered.

"Now, I understand that you have another few pieces you'll be working on with both of them in the next week or two?"

"Yes, right now I'm looking into a local bakery and will do the interview with Jessica at the end of next week, then gathering some background information on an extracurricular science program they're running out of a school in Potomac for Lauren. There's also an article on the Halloween carnival that I think we'll all be supporting this weekend."

Don nodded, writing again.

"Great, I'm glad you're keeping busy. I think you're aware that the final project for the internship will be a feature that you'll write all on your own. We do plan to publish the article in the magazine in the beginning of December, so I will be assigning that to you next week as well."

Emma nodded and smiled, although she felt her heart speed up in her chest.

"From what I've seen, and the feedback from your mentors, I believe you're ready for that. What do you think?"

"I hope so," Emma replied.

"And as I know you're aware, Jessica's retirement is approaching quickly. I think you've noticed that the two of them are frequently the busiest in the office, and we're looking to replace her. You will definitely be at the top of the pile, based on your work ethic and dedication so far."

"Thank you," Emma said, trying to hide her excitement. If her heart beat any louder, Don would be able to hear it from where he sat.

"Now there is one thing that I want you to keep in mind as you work your next couple weeks with Jessica and Lauren, and as you start working on the article by yourself."

"Yes?"

"It's something that I noticed could be improved both in your writing samples and your blog. You clearly have skill, and are very detail-oriented. But I think there is a key ingredient in that transition we talked about between your skills as a researcher and writer, and what will make your pieces something that people will want to read."

"What's that?" Emma asked.

Don smiled and pointed at his chest.

"Heart."

Chapter 25

The following morning, Emma awoke to her alarm and shut it off before sitting up, then pulled her shoulders back and rolled her neck around. She'd forgotten what it was like to work daily shifts where she had to stand up and bend over and lift rather than just sit at a computer all day. The stiffness in her neck wasn't bad, and she actually welcomed the deep sleep she got after being on her feet for so long at Mike's Coffee.

Emma slid out of bed, careful to avoid the kittens that seemed to be underfoot at all times. As soon as she started moving, they appeared, weaving between her legs as she moved from the bedroom to the kitchen.

"I'm going to start my coffee before I feed you. We've been over this," she told the kittens, who, as usual, ignored her. Their mother Daisy had warmed up to the idea of being an indoor cat, and spent most of her time on the kitchen bench in a sunny spot. Emma thought she would be able to tell the time based on where Daisy sat on the bench, as she moved to wherever the sun hit the cushion.

Emma ground beans for her coffee and filled the top with water, then set to getting the kittens' breakfast ready. She set down small bowls of food on the floor before filling Daisy's bowl and setting it beside the kitchen bench. The mother cat glanced at the bowl, then yawned and stretched before gliding across the bench and hopping down onto the floor. Daisy was by far the least needy or affectionate of the bunch, but Emma had grown to love the cat. She was independent and did exactly what she wanted all day, which Emma understood.

Emma made herself a bagel with cream cheese while she waited for her coffee to be ready, then filled a cup and took everything to the kitchen table to eat. While she sat, she pondered the plastic bag on the table in front of her.

The Halloween carnival was later that day, but Emma had gotten up early to turn the plastic bag filled with supplies from the craft store into a costume. Jessica and Lauren claimed that interviewing kids at the carnival would be more fun, and effective, if they were dressed up. Lauren was going as a witch, and Jessica said she was going as a giraffe. Emma had gone to the craft store between her internship and shift at the coffee shop, feeling creative, but as she sat in her kitchen, she wondered why she hadn't just bought a pre-made costume.

As Emma finished her last bite of bagel, there was a knock at the door. She squinted to read the clock on the microwave across the room before standing up.

"Just a second, Maxine," she called, then pulled open the door.

As usual, as soon as Emma saw Maxine, she felt underdressed. Maxine wore red pants with a buttoned red floral shirt, white shoes, and a white coat. Her red hair was, as usual, perfectly curled, and white flower earrings were clipped to her ears.

"Good morning. How did you know it was me?" Maxine asked, glancing at Emma's flannel pajamas.

"You're the only one who would come by before eight on a Saturday morning," Emma answered. "Can I get you a cup of tea?"

"No, thank you, I'll come by when you're back from the carnival," Maxine answered. "I was just coming by to ask if you could pick up a pumpkin or two for me."

"Sure thing. Any particular size?"

"They have a group specifically for baking, and I'd like two of those. Not the carving kind, and make sure there aren't any large warts or anything. I can pay you later today."

"Don't worry about it," Emma said, but Maxine waved her hands.

"Just let me know how much they are," Maxine said, then peered around Emma. "Doing some crafting today?'

Emma glanced back at the bag and saw that the craft store label was facing the door, otherwise she would've assumed that Maxine had people spying on her in town. It wouldn't surprise her.

"It's for my costume. Lauren and Jessica think it will help make us more approachable to the kids."

"Good thinking," Maxine said, nodding. "What are you going as?"

Emma considered not telling her, just to be difficult, but didn't see the point. "I'm going as a playing card. The queen of hearts," Emma said.

Maxine smiled. "That sounds perfect," she answered. "Well, I'll see you later tonight. Get a receipt for the pumpkins."

As Maxine descended down the stairs, Emma wondered if Maxine had somehow figured out the motivation behind the costume, or if she was just being nice.

"Now you're just being paranoid," Emma muttered, shaking her head as she closed the door.

Jessica crouched in front of a young girl dressed as a superhero who was holding her mother's hand and standing just behind her leg. Emma took a step back as Jessica turned her head and her pointed hat brushed Emma's legs. Emma's own costume had turned out better than she'd imagined. She'd cut hearts out of the felt she'd bought until she thought her fingers might cramp up, then hot glued them all over a long-sleeved white shirt she'd found in her closet and black tights. To make sure everyone understood her costume, she taped the queen of hearts playing card to a silver crown she'd purchased.

"Do you have a favorite Halloween candy?" Jessica asked the young girl.

"Chocolate!" the girl said, popping out from behind her mother for a second before sliding her thumb into her mouth and stepping back.

"That's my favorite, too," Jessica said, then groaned as she pushed against her knees and stood up again. "Thanks for talking to us," she said to the girl before thanking the parents before they turned away.

"She was a shy one," Emma said, and Jessica nodded.

"Sure lit up when I mentioned candy though," Jessica said. "How do you feel about splitting up? I might try to go find Lauren and see how her progress is going. Maybe you'll have more luck on your own."

"I don't know about that," Emma answered. "I can barely interview adults, let alone children."

As soon as Emma finished her sentence, she heard a familiar voice from behind her.

"Emma? Isn't that Emma?"

"It is! Emma!"

Emma turned to see two familiar blondes bounding her direction and smiled.

"Do you like my costume? I'm a fairy. But an evil one," Mia said.

"I'm the good fairy," Ally added.

"Who are you supposed to be?" Mia touched one of the felt hearts glued to Emma's sleeve.

"She's a heart, duh."

"Look at the card on her crown? Pretty sure she's the queen of hearts. *Duh.*"

"Looks like you're more popular than you think," Jessica commented, smiling.

"These are a couple friends of mine. Jessica, this is Mia and Ally. They're Jason's nieces. I imagine your dad and mom are around here somewhere?"

Mia started an eye roll that seemed to start in one eye and travel all the way across her face until it finished on Ally's.

"Dad wants to do the horse ride through the field, so he's buying tickets," Mia said, folding her arms across her chest.

"Lame, right?" Ally asked.

"I don't know, it could be fun," Emma said with a shrug. "I've never been on a horse."

"You haven't?"

Another familiar voice came from behind Emma, and she turned to see Jason, camera in hand, dressed as a scarecrow.

Emma shook her head. "Never," she answered.

"Oh my gosh, it's so easy. Plus the horses here go really slowly, and you're led around by a guide so you can't really go fast or anything," Mia said.

"You should come with us," Ally said, tugging on Emma's sleeve. "I mean, you'll see how lame it is, but still, I guess you might have fun."

"Sounds like it might be the right speed for someone who's never ridden before," Emma said. "But I'm working at the moment, so I might have to check it out later."

"Go ahead," Jessica interjected. "Plus you can add the experience to the article. Your first horse ride."

"Are you sure?"

"Absolutely," Jessica nodded. "I'm off to find Lauren anyway. Nice to meet you, girls," she added, then turned away.

"Well, sounds like I'm in," Emma said. "Where do we buy tickets?"

"Here, I'll show you," Mia said, grabbing Emma's hand.

"We'll both show you. Uncle Jason, are you coming?"

"Wouldn't miss it," he answered.

Emma allowed herself to be led by the girls, one on either side, with Jason following behind her. Surrounded by people who seemed to care about her, Emma almost let herself believe she could be a queen of hearts.

Twenty minutes later, Emma found herself gripping tightly to the reins connecting her hands to the bit in her horse's mouth, trying to use her feet in the stirrups to keep herself from sliding off.

"That helmet doesn't match your outfit at all," Mia said from her left.

"Yeah, you should've made them give you the red one," Ally agreed.

"Why'd you even get one if you didn't have to?" Mia asked. "In three years, I won't have to wear one."

"I thought it would be prudent since I've never ridden," Emma said, shifting in the saddle. The boys leading the horses couldn't have been much older than the twins, and Emma couldn't help but notice how frequently the girls glanced their way.

"You should ride at our friend Stephanie's house. She has like, eight horses. You can go way faster," Mia said.

"Or you could buy your own horse," Ally added, and Emma laughed.

"I think that might be jumping the gun a bit. Also, I'm not sure how much the kitties would like that."

"The kitties! I almost forgot. How are they?" Mia asked, her eyes wide, and Emma saw her sister nodding.

"They're great," Emma said. "Playful, fun, getting bigger every day. It's about time for me to get them another round of shots."

"You have to show us pictures when we're done," Mia said, and her sister nodded again.

"These girls talking your ear off?"

Emma turned to see Justin and Jason approach on their own horses beside them led by their own small team of teen boys.

"Not at all. They were asking about the kittens. Almost cats now, I guess," she added. She caught a look between the brothers before Justin cleared his throat.

"Justin, why don't you and the girls go ahead? I think I need to adjust one of my stirrups," Jason said.

"As long as my escort doesn't mind," Emma said, and the blonde boy at the front of her horse just smiled and shook his head.

"See you in a few," Justin said, waving before the three of them rode off slowly.

Emma watched as the three rode away, then turned to Jason and furrowed her eyebrows.

"Alright, what's really going on?" Emma asked.

"Why would you think something's going on?"

"I've been living next door to Maxine for over two months now. I know when there's more to the story."

Jason smiled, then waited as his brother and nieces rode even further away.

"Okay, you caught me," he said. "We can walk ahead, but slowly," he added to the boys guiding their horses.

"Aren't allowed any other speed," Jason's handler said, and the horses started moseying forward.

"I wanted to talk to you about your plans for the kittens," Jason said.

"Ah, are you thinking there might be two young red-heads who would be interested in giving them a home?"

"Not just thinking. Justin told me that they haven't stopped talking about them since they saw the pictures when you came for dinner."

Emma smiled. "I did promise more photos after our ride, so I imagine that will only ramp up their excitement."

"Justin wasn't sure if you were planning to keep them or not, so he has just been telling the girls 'no'. I let him know I'd ask you."

"I've been thinking about it, since I imagine it's about the time they can be fixed and rehomed. As much as I love them, I don't need that many. I was planning to keep Daisy, the mother, and one of her kittens. The black one tends to stick close to her, but the two grey ones like to play with each other. I can think of nothing better than to make sure those two have a good home."

"You would be making two young girls incredibly happy," Jason said. "And my brother would be willing to pay you for the vet costs or an adoption fee."

Emma nodded. "We'll work something out. When was he thinking?"

"Well, their birthday is just after Thanksgiving, if that works?"

"Works for me."

Emma looked forward at the girls in the distance. From where she sat, it looked like Mia and Ally were talking at once on either side of their father. Waiting at the end of the field was their mother, her bright blonde hair shining brightly in the sunlight.

"You look pretty happy over there," Jason said, and Emma sighed.

"I am," she said. "This is fun."

Chapter 26

"This is fun," Emma muttered to herself, hoping that if she said the words aloud, she might convince herself it was true. She closed her eyes and whispered it to herself again, then turned the key in the ignition.

The engine roared to life, and Emma twisted the temperature knob to the hottest setting and turned the heater on high. She couldn't remember ever using that combination of settings when she lived in San Diego, but even in the dead of winter, it rarely dipped below fifty degrees during waking hours. Since the temperature was so constant, Emma had barely even used the heater at all, which meant she didn't really know how well it worked.

Which was, it turned out, not very well at all.

She rubbed her hands against each other and blew hot air into them, then ducked out of her car and rushed back inside to finish making her lunch for the day. When September had faded into October and the temperature had started dropping, Emma was still doing her entire morning routine before heading out to the car. That process had changed as the weeks slid closer to November and Emma spent her entire drive to work shivering. By then, she had learned to start warming the car up before she was ready to leave for the day.

As Emma finished bagging her sandwich, the telephone rang.

"Thank you Maxine, but as I told you yesterday, and the day before that, I don't need your car today. My car works just fine."

"Good morning to you, too," Maxine huffed.

"Good morning," she said, putting her sandwich in a bag as her three growing kittens meowed for their breakfast. Emma grabbed their bowls and filled them with dry food before they tried to eat her tights, which they'd done before she learned to move faster.

"I'm telling you, it's going to snow today."

"You've been saying that for the past month," Emma said, but peered out the window to look at the sky. There was a thin layer of grey clouds overhead, but it didn't look any more menacing than it had the first week of October when Maxine first called about the snow.

"I'm telling you, it will. Plus I don't like the idea of you driving around in that old two-wheel drive heap over there while I have a perfectly good car with brand new snow tires in my garage, just waiting to get out."

Maxine didn't drive anymore, but she kept up the maintenance on an all-wheel drive car that she kept in the garage. Emma couldn't confirm it, but a small part of her suspected that Maxine got the car once she saw Emma pull into the neighborhood in her 'heap'.

"And I'm telling you, Maxine, I'll be fine. I put snow tires on last week, and I drive so slowly I think even you could beat me into the office."

They'd had this conversation so many times that if Emma didn't know any better, she'd think Maxine's memory was fading. But Emma had heard too many stories with details dating back to the mid-1900s to believe that Maxine would forget a conversation that happened every day.

"Well, you call me when you're on your way home, so I'll know if I need to send a search or not," Maxine conceded.

"Will do. Have a good day, Maxine," Emma answered, and hung up.

It was strange to have someone checking in on her constantly. Emma's mother worried when she was younger, especially when she'd started driving. But once Emma moved to college, the worry seemed to fade with the lack of contact between them. And Blake didn't seem to care too much where Emma was if she wasn't at home, which should have been another red flag for her. Meanwhile the woman across the street, who wouldn't stop worrying, probably already knew what color tights Emma was wearing that day.

Blake's obvious disinterest was just one more quality of his that she couldn't believe she'd let herself ignore, but she tried not to punish herself for it too badly anymore.

Emma pulled on her jacket, scarf, and hat, and grabbed her lunch before heading out the door. She shuffled quickly to the car, hoping it would be warm enough to at least take her hat off for the drive into work. It wasn't until she was inside the car with the doors shut that the engine shut off, and she could still see her breath when she exhaled.

"No, no, come on," she coaxed, once again turning the key in the ignition.

The first few times, the engine tried to turnover. On Emma's fourth try, she turned the key, and nothing happened – no engine noise, no clicking from a dead battery. Her San Diego car had finally given up and gone into hibernation for the winter. Emma hit the steering wheel with her hand, then sat in the freezing car, watching her breath make a frosted pattern on the windshield while she tried to figure out how to tell Maxine she was right without letting the old woman's ego swell too much.

At that moment, a small, perfect snowflake landed on the windshield directly on top of where Emma's breath had made a small circle. The snowflake melted into the tiniest puddle Emma could imagine before it was joined by four more. In her rearview mirror, Emma saw Maxine's front porch light turning off and on a few times.

Emma grabbed her lunch and exited the car. As the snow fell gently against her shoulders, she gave up on caring about Maxine's ego. She heard the phone ringing before her hand touched the front door, and answered on the third ring.

"It's snowing."

Emma could hear Maxine's gloating smile in her tone, even through the phone.

"Just because you were right on the thirtieth time saying it, doesn't make you right," Emma reminded her.

"All those other times were to convince you to take the car. This time I meant it," Maxine said.

"Mmhmm," Emma answered. "Well I appreciate the offer, and I think I'll have to take you up on it this morning."

"Wonderful!"

"Thank you again. I'll pay for gas, and whatever else you think I should owe you as a rental fee we can talk about after work. I'm starting to run late this morning though, so can I just head over now?"

"Oh, no need for payment, just gas is fine," Maxine answered. "I'll start it up in the garage to get it warmed up for you. That'll give you time to change your tights. That bright blue with the red shirt and white scarf makes you look a bit like the American Flag, don't you think?"

"Thanks again," Emma said, ignoring the last comment before she hung up. She shook her head, wondering why Maxine had ever quit the newspaper with how much she loved being involved in other people's lives. Maybe she could convince Don to offer Maxine a job writing a gossip column.

Still shaking her head, Emma walked into her bedroom to change into sturdier shoes to walk over to Maxine's in, when she caught her reflection in the mirror.

"Well, I'll be damned," she thought. Emma changed her shoes and grabbed a pair of black tights from her drawer, then stuffed them into her jacket pocket.

"No way I'm giving her the satisfaction of being right twice in one day," Emma said to herself, then charged back out into the cold.

Emma made it to work safely and barely on time, then changed her tights in the bathroom before she went to her desk and checked her email. She had spent a few minutes in the elevator lobby watching the snow coat the parking lot through the lobby window while her body warmed up. It had been getting colder every day, but something about watching the world transform into a layer of white really emphasized to Emma that she truly wasn't in San Diego anymore.

A knock behind her made Emma jump, and she turned to see Jason fill the entrance to the cubicles. He wore a dark green sweater that brought out his eyes and hugged his chest in a way that made Emma wonder how good of a pillow he would make. She tried not to notice, as he had become a good friend to her, but more and more she wondered if it would be worth ruining the friendship just to find out what his mouth tasted like.

"So, you ready for the big day?"

Thoughts of Jason's body and mouth dissipated, and Emma felt her heart pound in her chest.

"Yes. Maybe. I don't know," Emma said, shaking her head, and Jason laughed.

He was referring to her meeting with Don, where she was to discuss the first revision of her solo assignment for the magazine.

"Don't worry. You did most of the work on the Halloween article. You're all set."

Emma nodded and straightened her back.

"Yeah Emma, you're a rock star," Corinne said from the other side of the cubicle.

"You've worked on more articles than Corinne and I combined," Bev added.

"Thanks, ladies," Emma answered, and took a deep breath. "It's just weird with Lauren out of the office and Jessica gone."

Jessica's last day had been the previous Friday. With Thanksgiving just two weeks away, she wanted to quit with enough time to be stress-free by the holiday. Up until the moment Jessica left the building, Emma had convinced herself that she wasn't worried, that she was ready to write her first article on her own.

But as soon as Emma sat at her computer and saw the email from Don about her assignment, every insecurity and doubt that had ever existed within her had replaced any hope she could succeed. It was as though she'd spent months building a sandcastle, only to have a large rogue wave crash down and destroy it.

"Really, Emma," Jason said, pulling her from her imagination. "You'll do just fine."

The other interns smiled and nodded emphatically, but Emma suspected their enthusiasm was more directed at Jason than at her.

"Well, thanks for the support," Emma said, then turned back to her computer as Jason started to leave.

"I forgot to mention that I got a call from Maxine this morning," Jason said, reappearing at her cubical entrance.

"Did you?" Emma asked, although she wasn't surprised. Maxine had embraced the role of Montana Parent, and Emma knew that she had no choice but to accept the attention.

"She wants me to take you around the parking lot a few times at the end of the week, once the snow gets deep enough, to make sure you're comfortable driving."

Emma thought about protesting, telling Jason she didn't need his help, that she would be fine on her own. While she believed all of those things, she also knew it would only cause Maxine to pester Jason more, or to blame him if anything happened to Emma or the car.

"Fine," she sighed.

Jason smiled, then took a few steps closer to Emma's desk. He peered around it, then smiled wider.

"What?" Emma asked.

"Nothing," Jason said. "Let me know when works for you."

With that, he left her office.

Emma sat for a minute, confused, then looked down. It had looked like Jason was looking at her shoes, but why would he do that?

Then, as she stared down at the black tights covering her legs, Emma remembered – Maxine had called him.

"Damnit," she said, crossing her legs before pulling out her notebook.

"What? Is Maxine a relative?" Corinne asked from behind her, but Emma just shook her head.

"Something like that," she muttered.

"Ugh, that's like my parents. Always wanting to get involved in everything," Corinne said before turning back around.

Emma thought she should be annoyed, but she couldn't help but smile.

Chapter 27

"It's good."

Don set the stapled sheets of Emma's first article down on his desk in front of him and took off his reading glasses.

"Good?" Emma asked.

It was Wednesday morning, and Emma had waited as long as she could manage before emailing her first article to Don. She still planned to interview people, but since the thought terrified her, she thought maybe she could try a version without interviews. Emma had sent the article to Don without the interview, hoping he would tell her it was perfect as it was and that she could move onto her next story.

Based on the way Don used "good", the same way a parent might describe the first batch of cookies their child ever made, Emma knew she wouldn't be skipping back to her office anytime soon.

"Don't look so terrified," Don said, reading Emma's face. "The research is all there, and the background is thorough. Really impressive in terms of the factual aspects."

"But?"

Emma could feel her confidence slipping away. She was so excited about this article. It was her first chance to prove to herself that she could make it as a real writer on her own, that she hadn't made the biggest mistake of her life by moving to Montana, that Blake was wrong. Somehow, her entire future hung on how she did on this article. Logically, she knew she couldn't be perfect on the first iteration, but her confidence was so fragile that she was afraid any amount of negativity could send her into a tailspin.

"But I think you know what's missing," Don said, raising his eyebrows at her.

Emma paused and bit her lip before letting out a breath.

"Heart?"

Don pointed his finger at Emma and nodded his head once.

"Yes. The skeleton is there, the backbone. But there isn't any life to it. Have you talked to Chuck?"

Chuck was the owner of the business Don had assigned to Emma for her article. She had his name and phone number on her desk. She'd dialed the beginning of his number so many times throughout the week that it was ingrained into her brain.

"I was planning to talk to him yesterday, but I ended up digging into the research instead."

"That part is definitely solid. Now you just need to put Chuck into it somewhere."

Emma nodded, but stayed quiet.

After a pause, Don tilted his head.

"Something wrong?"

She debated telling him she was fine, but two things stopped her. First, she would never grow or improve at this job by hiding behind her fears. And second, Don might need glasses for reading an article in front of him, but he had no trouble reading Emma. Denial would just send his reporter brain into overdrive.

"I don't know how to do an interview on my own," Emma said. "I'm not as good at talking to people as Lauren and Jessica are. Everything I've ever written has been about objects and processes, not people. I've had practice with them, but never on my own. Manuals don't need heart. I guess I'm just not sure if I know how to do what you're asking without help."

Don smiled.

"Emma, you've been learning from Lauren and Jessica for two months now. They've both told me how well you've done, and how much you've learned. This will be your first time on your own, but it's just the same as when you all went together. You just need practice. The groundwork for the article is there. And I've known Chuck and his family for decades. He's quirky, but just about the nicest man you'll ever meet. Chatty, too. Ask him half a question and he'll spend an hour answering you."

Emma took a deep breath and nodded. She wasn't convinced, but Don seemed to have faith in her despite her own trepidation.

"You'll want to catch him before lunch, though. He eats at the same time every day, so at least that way he'll have a reason to stop talking. If you wait until after lunch, he'll keep you there until sundown."

"Got it," Emma said, rising from Don's guest chair.

"And you won't be totally alone. Remember to grab Jason on your way out for pictures for the article," Don said.

Of course, Emma thought to herself, but she only smiled and walked out of Don's office.

Half an hour later, Emma found herself staring into the open mouth of a grizzly bear, its skin hanging loosely around the sharpest teeth she'd ever seen.

Chuck's Taxidermy was just a ten minute drive from the office, and Jason had offered to drive since he knew the way. There was a brief moment in the parking lot when Emma tried to decide whether or not she should fake an illness and force herself to reschedule, but pulled herself together. She spent the entire drive to Chuck's taking deep breaths and reminding herself that she was going into an interview, not a root canal. Thankfully, Chuck was just as conversational as Don had promised.

If not more so.

"We put the teeth into the body first. Once the hide is on, we pull the lips around the teeth and trim them up so they're nice and tight," Chuck explained, pulling on the loose lip skin.

Emma flinched as the camera shutter clicked right next to her face, and Jason smiled as he pulled the camera down. Researching taxidermy from her office was one thing. But Emma had only just gotten used to owning cats; seeing a large animal, even a dead one, from this range was something else altogether.

"So most of your projects are from hunters?" Emma asked, her pen poised above her notebook in a way that made her feel so official she could have exploded. Although with how much Chuck talked, she made a note to buy herself a tape recorder to save her wrist from future arthritis.

"Mostly," Chuck answered, nodding.

He swiped his rough fingers underneath a weathered ball cap and scratched the sparse white hairs on top of his head, then pulled on the brim to settle the hat back down.

"I get the occasional household pet, cats and dogs, but mostly it's mounts. I also run a small school for people who want to learn. It's a dying art, but people are still interested in it."

Emma listened and wrote as much as she could as Chuck delved into the various animals currently on display in his shop – multiple deer and elk, and even one large moose head he claimed to have shot himself. His knowledge and passion for his craft was so clear that Emma scolded herself for doing the interview last. She could have skipped the research altogether and just come straight to an expert.

As it neared lunchtime, Emma had ten pages of notes and a cramp in her fingers, and had learned more about taxidermy and Chuck's business than she already had for the article. But she still felt as though she was missing the heart, the life of the story. She saw Chuck check his watch and she began to panic.

"Looks like I'm about ready for lunch. Was there anything else you needed?"

Emma's mind went blank, and she felt her lungs tighten. Chuck turned towards the door and took a step towards it while Jason took another photo of one of Chuck's completed mounts.

A bear's teeth is not heart, she told herself. Where was the queen of hearts now?

"Heart," she blurted out, and Chuck stopped walking and turned around. Emma saw Jason bring his camera down from his face as he tilted his head, but said nothing.

"Sorry, I mean," Emma cleared her throat, then glanced at the window beside the door. "Is that a new window sign?"

Chuck glanced back at the window, and when he turned back at Emma, he smiled.

"Good eye," he said.

"Why don't we take a few shots of you beside it?" Emma suggested, glancing at Jason.

"Sure thing," Chuck answered, and lumbered his large body towards the front door.

Emma followed closely behind, and just as they reached the front, she felt Jason's breath against her cheek.

"Breathe," he whispered.

Chuck held the door open in front of them, and Jason let Emma walk outside first. She took a deep breath of the fresh air outside as Jason positioned Chuck in front of the painted window with his moniker on it.

"So, how new are we talking?" Emma asked as Jason stood a few feet away from them on the sidewalk snapping photos.

"Just last week," Chuck answered, beaming. "The old one was so old and faded you could only read it from three feet away. It was hard to watch the old one get scraped off, but the new looks beautiful."

"Why was the first one hard to get rid of?" Emma asked.

"Well, my father helped me put the first one on thirty years ago. I know the memory is still in my head, but something about having something around that he touched just felt good."

"I can understand that," Emma said. "He isn't still with us?"

Chuck shook his head, leaning against the window with a sigh.

"It's been five years, and sometimes I still find myself calling into the other room for him to bring me the scraper."

"He worked with you?" Emma asked. Don had been right, Chuck was easy to talk to. She tried to keep herself focused, especially since moments earlier she could barely breathe. She glanced at Jason, but he was focused on his camera. He did seem to be smiling, though.

"We opened the shop together when he retired. I went to school for economics over in Washington and stayed in Seattle for a decade or so working in an office. Then my mom got sick, so I quit and came home. She made it another two years, but then it was just me and Dad."

"Wow," was all Emma could think to say. She tucked her notebook into her back pocket and stepped closer to Chuck.

"Dad took it pretty hard. My mom's happiness was all he ever cared about, and he was just about to retire. We'd always gone hunting and fishing together when I was a kid, so that first year home I worked in a small office and took him out to the woods as often as I could. We met a guy after one trip who mounted an elk for us, and my dad got fascinated by the process. There's a taxidermy school in Eureka, about three hours north of here, and he and I enrolled together. A few years later, we opened up shop, and it finally seemed like he had a reason to get up in the morning."

"That's incredible that you gave up your whole life to be with your dad," Emma said, then heard the click of Jason's camera.

Chuck shrugged. "He was my dad. He would have given up his life many times over if it would've brought me joy. Plus it ended up working out for the both of us. I met my wife here when she came in with a boyfriend."

"A boyfriend?" Emma teased.

Chuck blushed. "I didn't steal her. She just kept coming in to visit after the job was done, and eventually she asked me out. So it was all her."

"How about your dad? Did he ever remarry?"

"Oh yeah. He met his second wife, Martha, about ten years after we opened when she brought in her cat. One of the best jobs my dad had ever done was mounting that cat, trying to impress Martha. He kept it after she passed, he was so attached to it. I think I have it here somewhere, if you'd want to see it before my wife gets here for lunch?"

"No thanks," Emma said, trying not to think of her own kittens back at home as Jason's camera clicked away.

Chapter 28

Two days later, Emma found herself again riding the elevator down to the parking lot alone with Jason. Emma didn't know what Jason was working on, but she had written and rewritten her article so many times that she thought she had it memorized. Even with Chuck's additional details, Emma didn't think the story had the 'heart' that Don asked for, and she was feeling discouraged.

It didn't help that Jason had spent the entire elevator ride reminding her that Maxine had instructed him to show Emma a few pointers in snow driving.

"I can figure it out, thanks," Emma said as they pushed out into the cold afternoon air. "Plus I only have an hour until I need to be at the coffee shop."

"I'm just offering to help. I think the last time it snowed in Southern California was almost forty years ago, and you definitely wouldn't have been old enough to drive back then. Or alive, even."

"One of my school teachers talked about it I think," Emma answered, tucking her scarf tighter around her neck as she picked up her pace to the car. It had snowed over six inches throughout the day, and was supposed to double overnight. The parking lot and surrounding roads had been plowed, and Emma wondered fleetingly what her driveway would look like by morning and whether or not she'd be able to get out of it.

One thing at a time, she thought.

"Can I just give you a few pointers?" Jason pleaded.

"Really, I'm fine," Emma said.

"I know you're fine," he said, stepping closer to her. "You're an article-writing, coffee-making, horse-riding, cat-owning badass," he said.

Emma bit her lip as Jason took another step closer, and Emma could almost feel his breath warm her frozen nose.

"I just want to make sure you're safe," he said, then smiled. "Plus, Maxine made me promise to help you. She'd never forgive me if you slid off the road."

"Maxine," Emma groaned, shaking her head. The combination of Jason's closeness and Maxine's meddling was making her head spin, and she decided that regardless of Jason's offer, she shouldn't drive anywhere just yet.

"Fine," she said, and Jason's eyes lit up.

"Fantastic. There's an empty lot at the end of the street. We can practice without worrying about hitting anything."

"You think I'll be that bad?" Emma asked. Jason's car was clear at the other side of the empty lot.

"Not at all," he answered. "But we're going to have some fun, and I don't want anyone else's car to pay for it." With that, he extended his arm towards Emma's car. She took her keys from her purse and unlocked it, then hopped inside and turned the heater on, wondering what type of teaching Jason was going to be giving her.

Twenty minutes later, Emma found herself in Maxine's car, driving slowly through the empty, snow-covered lot down the street from her office.

"Okay, now really punch it, and turn the wheel hard to the right."

Emma pushed on the gas, but didn't think five miles an hour could be called 'punching it'.

Jason had spent ten minutes as the driver, and Emma had squealed and laughed beside him as he spun the car through the ice and snow in the parking lot. Now in the driver's seat, she found herself reserved and terrified.

"You don't drive this slowly when you head home, do you?" Jason asked.

Emma shook her head.

"No, but the roads have been plowed really well, and there's always someone ahead of me."

Emma stared out to a patch in the lot that she knew was covered in slick ice, and pressed on the brakes.

"I promise, nothing is going to happen," Jason said. "The parking lot is empty, there's nothing you can hit."

"I don't know," Emma said, watching the snow gather onto the hood of the car before melting from the heat of the engine.

"Really, it'll be fun. Plus you need to know how the car will react in icy conditions."

"I don't know," Emma said again.

"Emma-"

"No!"

Emma saw Jason flinch next to her, and turned to him, but said nothing. They sat next to each other with the engine running.

"Emma," Jason said. "We were having fun a minute ago, and you've been driving through the snow all week. You know that nothing bad can happen to you in this parking lot. What's this really about?"

Emma bit her lip and watched the snow fall outside.

"I'm not sure I know how to do this," she said.

"Driving?" Jason asked, and Emma shook her head.

"I don't know if I can do it on my own. I don't know if I can find the heart."

She looked over at Jason, who was looking back at her with a blank expression.

"I'm afraid you've lost me."

Emma looked back out at the falling snow and sighed.

"Don liked my research, but he thought my original draft didn't have enough heart. I've been rewriting the article since we talked to Chuck on Wednesday, but I don't think I have it. I'm not even sure what I got from Chuck was heart."

"Emma, the man told you his entire life story. You cracked his shell. How did you even do it? How did you know there was a story behind the new sign?"

Emma shrugged. "For one, I don't think Chuck has much of a shell. But honestly I didn't know for sure, it was just the first thing I saw."

"But you kept pressing him. Why?" Jason asked.

"I don't know, really. The way he talked about it made it sound like it was more than just a paint job."

"And it was," Jason said. "*You* found that. You need to give yourself more credit."

"Maybe," Emma said, then sighed again.

"Can I ask you a question?" Jason asked, and Emma turned her head towards him.

He was watching her with one of those looks she'd gotten used to, but still didn't understand. Emma loved having Jason as a friend, but sometimes he gave her that look, a combination of caring and amusement and something else she couldn't place, and it rattled the walls restraining her inhibitions. There was something in his eyes that lit a fire in her.

"Tell me if I'm crossing a line here," he continued, "but does this sudden wave of doubt have anything to do with your dad? Or maybe Blake?"

Emma looked back out the window and considered Jason's question.

"I don't know, maybe," Emma said after a long silence. "Even after everything I've been doing, how hard I've been working, how happy I think I am, there's this voice in my head that tells me that I should try harder, that I should be better. At the same time, the voice tells me that there isn't any point in trying because my dreams aren't worth anything, and I'll never achieve them anyway." She tucked her hair behind her ear and leaned her head against the cold window. "Sometimes it's my father's voice, sometimes it's Blake's. But mostly, it just sounds like mine."

Emma looked out the front windshield and watched the snow fall. It didn't rain often in San Diego, but when it did, it was often accompanied by wind and traffic jams. Everything about it was loud. But as she sat in her car with Jason watching the snow transform the world around them into a land of soft white, she was struck by how quiet it was. She thought such a big change would be loud and obnoxious, but it was just peaceful.

"I don't want to add another voice to your head, but maybe you should just tell them all to shut the hell up," he said.

Emma turned towards him as he continued.

"You can't ignore all the good and believe that you're the sum of all the bad things you think about yourself. It doesn't work that way."

"But-"

"But nothing," Jason said, surprising Emma with his stern tone. "You're smart and brave, and deserve all the good things you want for yourself. You just have to be willing to keep trying."

Jason put his warm hand on her arm, and Emma felt a chill run down her spine despite the heat pumping from the vents in front of her.

"Okay, I think I'm ready," Emma said, despite how not-ready she felt.

Jason drew his hand away and repeated his earlier instructions. Emma pushed hard on the gas, and grabbed the wheel as tightly as she could. While Jason laughed beside her and directed her motions, she tried to ignore the heat still emanating from the spot on her arm. She reminded herself that he had been comforting her, that it didn't mean anything. He was her friend, nothing more.

After another few reckless laps around the parking lot, Emma decided it was time to make her way to the coffee shop, and drove Jason back to the magazine parking lot.

"I feel confident in reporting to Maxine that you will make it home safely," he said, smiling, and Emma smacked him on the arm.

"It'd be funnier if I knew you weren't kidding about reporting back," Emma said.

"She cares about you," Jason said with a shrug. He opened his mouth to say something else, but smiled instead.

"Thanks again for your help this week. With talking to Chuck, and... this." She gestured to the car, but hoped he knew that she meant more than just the driving.

"Anytime," Jason said. "I think you're a great writer, and that you'll do just fine. You're so much more than you give yourself credit for."

Emma nodded, trying to believe it herself, while Jason pulled on his door handle. She shivered as a rush of cold air pushed into the cab. She expected Jason to leave immediately, but he paused.

"What do you think about me?" he said in a low voice, and she pulled back, surprised.

"I think," Emma stammered. His cheeks flushed as the cold air hit his skin, and the stubble on his chin straightened with the goosebumps. There was so much she wanted to say, but despite his pep talk, the voice in Emma's head whispered doubt into her ears.

"I think you're a good photographer," she said. "And a really great friend."

Jason tilted his head and nodded, his eyebrows furrowing as the look in his eyes changed again.

"Thank you," he said, then pushed the door fully open and stepped into the snow. "I hope it isn't too crazy at the coffee shop today. Drive safe," he said, then shut the door behind him.

Emma watched him in her rearview mirror as he walked behind her car towards his truck. She saw him shake his head as he reached the back, then pull himself up into the cab of his truck. As his headlights turned on behind her, Emma glanced at her reflection in the rearview mirror. Her cheeks were still 'chubby as a chipmunks', as her dad used to tell her, and her hair was still the same boring brown. Someone like Jason couldn't possibly desire someone like her, could he?

As Jason pulled away from the curb and drove down the road, Emma was stunned to realize that she finally understood the look on his face, the one he had given her just before he left her car and walked out into the cold.

It was hurt.

CHAPTER 29

"So you have a crush on Jason. What's so wrong with that?" Maxine rolled out a pie crust on the kitchen table as Emma chopped apples across from her.

"I didn't say I had a crush on him," she protested.

"No. You said it was nice he spent time with you yesterday afternoon, how much fun you had driving in the parking lot with him, how good of a listener he is. How concerned that you might have hurt his feelings somehow."

"That doesn't mean I have a crush on him," Emma said, and Maxine huffed.

"Emma, you've been here nearly six months now-"

"Not even three," Emma corrected.

"Fine, three," Maxine said, continuing to roll the dough out more vigorously than Emma would have expected was possible at her age. Although why Emma continued to be surprised by anything Maxine could do was the real mystery.

"Three months, and you've liked him from the beginning. From that first dance."

"I thought he was good-looking, obviously. And now that I've gotten to know him, I know that he's a fantastic photographer, and kind, and clearly loves his family. But-"

Maxine raised the roller in her hand and pointed it at Emma.

"But nothing. If you use that old Blake excuse I will smack you with this roller. You've been over him since a week after you crossed state lines, and don't try to tell me otherwise. I know you like to use that as your safety blanket, but I'm not having it."

Emma paused with her mouth open, her hand frozen mid-cut through a chunk of apple. Maxine waited, still holding out the rolling pin like a sword she wasn't afraid to use.

"You're right," she admitted, and Maxine finally lowered the weapon back to the pie crust dough. "I think I am finally over Blake. I don't agree that I was over him after just a week, but I think I'm over him now."

Maxine nodded.

"Then what's the problem?"

"With having a crush on Jason?" Emma tossed the last chunks of apple into the large bowl in front of her and stirred them into a sugar and spice mixture with a large wooden spoon as she thought.

What was the problem with having a crush on Jason? The amazing photographer and person who, incidentally, was one of the sexiest men she had ever seen up close, who treated her kindly and never made her feel small?

"He's too good for me," she said with a shrug, then looked down into the bowl to scrape the unmixed sugar from the sides of the bowl.

With her head down, she didn't see the roller coming down until it slammed onto the table directly in front of her face.

"Whoa!" she said, dropping the spoon in surprise. "What was that for?" Emma was startled by the noise the roller made when it contacted the table, but not as surprised as she was to see the look on Maxine's face.

Maxine was furious.

"That was to knock some sense into that head of yours," Maxine said, shaking the roller at Emma again, as though it was an extension of her finger.

"I know you and your parents had issues, and I know somehow you convinced yourself that being with someone like Blake who doesn't love or respect you is what you deserve."

Emma opened her mouth, but Maxine continued.

"Do you remember when you moved here, you told me that falling out of love with Blake was like paint fading on a fence? How you didn't notice the change until you got some distance?"

Maxine waited, and Emma nodded.

"Well I'm telling you, the same thing has happened to you, in reverse. You've been changing since the moment you crossed state lines. You aren't the same girl who let her boyfriend discourage her from her dreams. You aren't the same writer, or the same friend. You're finally figuring out what you're capable of, figuring out how to love yourself for who you are. Your heart deserves a chance to go after what it wants. *You* deserve it. You've been painting your fence, and let me tell you, from where I stand, it's beautiful."

Maxine waited while Emma sat and stared at her bowl of apples. Eventually, she put aside her rolling pin, and Emma watched as Maxine deftly maneuvered the dough into the waiting pan and pressed it into the edges.

Emma wanted to fight back against Maxine, to tell her that nothing she said was true. She wasn't all that brave, and she'd never been the smartest in any class of hers. She had put herself through college and graduated, but many of her peers had. Sure, maybe the move to Montana could be considered brave, but only because it hadn't fallen apart yet. Emma might not get the job that Jessica had vacated when the internship was over, and then that supposed courage would just look like pure stupidity.

The caring part, Emma found, she couldn't really argue. Emma absolutely cared about Maxine; she felt closer to her neighbor than she felt even to Marcy, who she'd known for nearly a decade. And Emma had cared about her parents so much, despite how absent they had both been. She'd spent her childhood trying to get her father to care back, and her early twenties wondering how to get over losing her mother to a new family. Emma had believed Blake cared about her. Emma had felt that, like her father, Blake's criticisms showed his concern and love for her.

But here, sitting in Maxine's dim kitchen and watching the woman slice pie crust into lattice strips, Emma slowly felt a small empty hole she'd long forgotten about begin to fill in her heart. This woman, whom she'd only known a few months, wanted her to be happy so badly it made her angry. She wanted Emma to believe in herself, and to want more for herself than what she thought she deserved. More than anything, Emma wanted to believe that she was the woman Maxine thought she was. Emma wanted the life for herself that Maxine apparently thought she deserved.

It made her feel good.

"I'm not sure I know how to paint my fence," she said.

"You do," Maxine said. "Your heart is already on the right path, you just need to stop fighting it and keep moving forward."

"I don't know what that means, but I guess I'll take your word for it."

"You should. Now pass me that bowl."

Emma pushed the bowl of sugary apples towards Maxine, who piled them on top of her crust and spread them out evenly before carefully laying the dough for the lattice across the top. Even raw, the pie looked delicious.

"When do we get to eat it?" Emma asked as Maxine set it into her oven.

"Oh, this pie isn't for us. This is for Arthur," she said, then tossed Emma a rag.

"Who's Arthur?" she asked, as she began wiping the errant flour and sugar from the table.

"Oh, you'll see him in the morning when you give him the pie."

"Maxine, what are you talking about?"

Maxine sighed and put her hand on her hip. "It's the first snow, and our driveways are both getting to the point where they're more of an obstacle course than flat ground. So Arthur will be by in the morning. Just make sure to be up by six-thirty."

"On a Sunday?" Emma asked.

"Yes, on a Sunday," Maxine said. "And from the sound of things, you've got so much going on in that head of yours that you probably won't sleep much anyway."

Emma shook her head. Even her own diary would have trouble competing with how well Maxine seemed to know Emma.

"Now," Maxine continued, "tell me more about this article of yours that you're so worried about."

Emma knew that once Maxine changed the subject, there was no going back. Any protests she wanted to make regarding her feelings for Jason would fall on deaf ears. So she pushed her curiosity aside for the moment, and tried to focus on talking about her article, while the appealing scent of the pie for Arthur filled her nostrils.

CHAPTER 30

As Maxine had predicted, Emma was awake long before six-thirty. She had tried to make sense of her thoughts on work and on Jason by writing in her journal, but after three pages of questions to herself that she couldn't answer, she had finally turned off the light and tried to sleep. After a long night of tossing and turning, Emma stood with a cup of coffee in her kitchen, watching the snow continue to fall in the dark morning.

She heard a loud rumble, and at six-thirty exactly, a tractor and plow rumbled into her yard. Bundled in her new winter coat and boots, Emma trotted out to Arthur's truck and handed him the wrapped pie, which he tucked into a compartment underneath his seat. Emma thanked him before running back inside, where her fire was blazing. She watched from the window as Arthur efficiently cleared a path from her car to the road, then drove across the street to Maxine's.

By ten-thirty, Emma had finished a pot of coffee and made herself a full breakfast of eggs and bacon. The dishes that had been piling in the sink were washed and put away, she had folded all of her clean clothes, and every surface she could reach was free of any speck of dust. She wasn't normally a tidy person, but procrastination had a way of motivating her.

When she'd run out of things to do around the house and couldn't convince her body to walk out into the freezing snow, Emma grabbed her laptop and sat down at her kitchen table. She opened the article on Chuck and his shop, and stared at the blinking cursor. She read aloud what she had written Friday, and nearly cried at how terrible it sounded.

"I don't know what I'm doing," she told the kitchen, and rested her head on the table. For the next two hours, she tried rearranging the paragraphs, removing and adding details, but nothing she did seemed right. The harder she worked at the article, the farther away she felt she was getting from putting in the 'heart' that Don said he wanted.

Emma's growling stomach finally made her take a break for lunch, and as she heated up a can of soup on the stove, she wondered how disappointed Don would be that Jessica was gone, and that Emma wasn't fit to be hired as her replacement. How had Marcy convinced her to move out here? How had Emma convinced herself that she would ever be successful?

Emma poured her soup into a bowl and turned off the stove as she spiraled into a sea of self-doubt and sadness. Maxine wasn't right about her. Emma wasn't any different than the scared, insecure girl who had left California. She was just the same, except now, she was also cold.

Out the window, the low rumble of a car engine distracted her. She looked out the kitchen window to see a car stop on the road between Maxine's driveway and her own. Someone jumped out of the car and shuffled up to Maxine's door with the car running, the exhaust pushing plumes of smoke into the cold air. Emma watched as Maxine opened the door to the stranger, and after a few moments, Maxine pointed to Emma's cabin.

Emma stepped back from the window. The stranger walked through the snow back down the steps and to his car. He pulled forward and turned into Emma's freshly-plowed driveway.

Back across the street, Maxine stood in her still open doorway, wrapped in a heavy blanket. Emma felt her heart beat faster. Whatever was coming her way, it was something Maxine was willing to stand in the cold for.

Emma walked to her doorway as she heard the car approach, and the subsequent silence when the engine shut off. She heard nothing for a few moments as the stranger walked through the snow, then loud thuds as heavy boots hit her porch steps. The kittens, who had been sleeping in their beds in the kitchen, jumped at the noise, then trotted into the living room to lay by the fire.

The footsteps stopped just outside Emma's door, but no one knocked. She contemplated grabbing the cordless phone in case she needed to call the police, but decided it was unnecessary. Maxine wouldn't knowingly send trouble Emma's way.

Emma reconsidered that thought when she heard a knock and opened the door to find Blake standing on the other side.

"Emma, hi," he said.

Blake leaned forward and gave Emma a quick hug. She left her arms at her sides, then folded them in front of her when Blake pulled back. She stood in her doorway, halfway between the warmth of the fire and the chill seeping in from outside, wondering what the hell Blake was doing on her porch.

"Can I come in?" he asked when Emma didn't offer.

"I'm not sure," she said, and watched with some satisfaction as Blake frowned, then drew his coat tighter around him.

"What are you doing here?" she asked.

Blake shifted on his feet, and Emma wasn't sure if it was from the discomfort of her response or from the cold.

"I wanted to see you," he answered, lifting up his mouth in the thin smile that had first attracted Emma to him. She originally considered it mysterious and sexy. Now, she just saw it as a ploy for him to convince her to do what he wanted.

"You haven't wanted to see me in months. You haven't talked to me in almost that long. And suddenly you flew to Montana in winter because of some sudden urge?" Emma shook her head. "Aren't you dating someone else?" she added.

Blake dropped his smile and shook his head.

"We broke up," he said, then took a step closer and lowered his voice. Again, it was a move that used to turn her on. "It wasn't going to work out. She just wasn't what I wanted. She wasn't you." He reached his hand to her cheek and ran it down her jaw before looking into her eyes.

Emma tilted her head as though to crack her neck, and Blake dropped his hand.

"But 'not being me' should be a good thing," Emma answered. "Because you dumped *me*, you said being with *me* didn't make you happy."

Blake shook his head.

"Emma, we were together for three years. We had some great times. I think I was just getting bored at the end. You clearly were too," Blake said, gesturing towards Emma and her cabin. "You had to make this crazy move out of state just to spice things up. Now you can come back refreshed. Like I said before, I'm sure you could get your old job back. We could start over, go back to before we fell apart. Things could go back to the way they were. Back to when you didn't live in a cabin in zero-degree weather," he added with a laugh.

Emma thought about asking where Blake's sudden change of heart came from, but she found that she didn't care.

She thought about yelling at him for all the times he had discounted her dreams and feelings, wanted to list all the times he'd hurt her and made her feel less than she was. And even now, using her as a backup plan should have made her furious. Instead, she felt calm, and she smiled.

"Thank you," she said.

Blake smiled back tentatively.

"For coming out here? Does that mean-" He took another step towards her, but Emma held up her hand.

"You were right, what you said when you left. I wasn't happy," Emma explained. "But it wasn't just with us, it was with myself. I was unhappy with my whole life. I'd convinced myself that I needed to stay in a job that I hated because it was the smart thing, because my dreams were just fantasies. I believed that I deserved to be with a man who made me feel insecure, who belittled those dreams."

Blake opened his mouth, but again, Emma held up her hand to him.

"Now, I know better," she said, and straightened her back. "I have people who believe that my dreams aren't nothing. They believe in *me*. And I'm finally starting to believe in myself, too. And it's because I made this crazy decision that I have all of those things and that I'm reaching towards happiness. Dumping me was the best thing you could have done for me, and I appreciate you for that."

Blake remained silent as Emma took a step back into the house.

"So thank you, Blake," she said, raising her hand up to her door. "Now get the hell off my porch."

Emma caught only a glimpse of the surprise on Blake's face before she slammed the door and threw the lock. The noise had again disturbed the kittens, and Emma stood motionless in the kitchen as they circled her feet.

It was a few minutes before Emma heard Blake's footsteps descend her porch, then another minute before the engine of his car started. She waited until the engine noise faded completely before opening the top half of her split door to poke her head outside.

Her driveway was empty, and across the road, Emma saw Maxine nod her head twice before moving inside and shutting her own door.

Emma closed the top of the door and latched it before reaching down to scratch each of the kittens on the head. She walked back to the table to her open laptop and the blinking cursor.

"I believe in myself," she said aloud, then smiled.

Chapter 31

"Hmm," Don mumbled again.

By Emma's count, it was the sixth time he'd done it since she'd been called into his office. It was nearly noon on Monday afternoon, the time Don usually left for lunch. She'd worked all day Sunday on her rewrite for the piece on Chuck's Taxidermy, and had sent it to Don first thing Monday morning. By noon, she'd assumed she wouldn't hear anything until Wednesday, but just before lunch he'd called her into his office so they could go through it together.

Apparently 'going through it together' meant Don read and mumbled while Emma watched, quietly trying not to have a heart attack.

"Well," Don said, removing his reading glasses as he peeled his gaze from the computer screen and focused on Emma.

In the short pause between when he finished the article and started speaking again, Emma managed to mentally pack her bags and drag her pathetic, failing self back to California.

"That's what I was looking for," he said with a smile.

"Really?" Emma's heart was pounding as she felt a glimmer of hope.

"Really. Chuck's backstory is what makes the article interesting, gives it the heart I was looking for."

"Thank you," she beamed, allowing her brain to throw her mental luggage back into the cabin she had begun to call home.

"I'm off to lunch, so just forward this off to Carl and he'll create the layout with Jason's photos before we do a final edit. Other than that, have a great rest of your day."

"Okay," Emma said, rising from Don's guest chair and heading back towards her own office. Her brain was swirling.

The words 'final edit' and 'nice work' kept racing through her mind. She had written something that someone else thought was good enough to put through a final edit before it went into a magazine. An article that had heart, and a story.

Before going back to her desk, Emma went to the women's restroom and shut the door behind her. She leaned against the wall, staring at herself in the mirror, conflicted between smiling and crying. The combination of Blake's surprise visit and their conversation, along with Don's approval of her article were overwhelming.

She had embraced failure, as Jessica would say. Suddenly the dreams she'd always held in her heart were happening, and Emma couldn't believe it. She took another few minutes to regain her composure, then sat at her computer and forwarded her article to Carl, along with the photos Jason sent her for the article.

Jason.

He had smiled at her politely that morning, but didn't say anything. Emma read through the rest of her emails to make sure there wasn't anything else she needed to do before starting her shift at the coffee shop, then packed up her bag and shut down her computer. She bundled herself in a mound of clothing to prepare for the short, but freezing, walk out to her car, then shut down her computer and walked towards Jason's office. She hadn't seen him since that morning, and wanted to talk to him. She wanted to thank him again for his help with the article, but also to ask him if they could talk.

Emma knocked lightly on his door and shifted her purse on her arm, waiting.

"He's out the rest of the week," Don's voice said from behind her. He carried his briefcase and wore a sweater that was too light for Emma even in spring in San Diego, let alone the middle of a Montana winter.

"Oh?" Emma asked. "On vacation?"

Don shrugged. "Didn't say. He came in this morning for an hour or so, then left. He hasn't taken a week off for as long as I can remember."

"Oh," Emma said again.

"You on your way out?" he asked, and Emma nodded. "I'll walk you to your car, then."

Emma followed Don to the elevator, and they made light conversation while they waited for the elevator to rumble its way up to their floor. She glanced back at Jason's closed door and wondered where he'd gone, and why he didn't say goodbye.

And when the elevator doors opened and Don waited for Emma to board, she realized that there was one more fear she needed to confront before she could feel complete.

Chapter 32

As Don had mentioned, Jason was out of the office the entire week. With each passing day, Emma felt his absence more and more. He wasn't at work, and he didn't surprise her at the coffee shop.

Originally, she had planned to wait until he got back into the office the following Monday to talk to him. She had thought she would ask him out for coffee or dinner to let him know that she thought of him as more than a friend. It was a different strategy than she ever would have used back in her old life in San Diego, as she never would have been the one to make the first move. But it also didn't quite fit in with her new self, either. Just asking Jason for coffee still had the hints of the old, timid Emma.

On Friday evening, after work, Emma sat in her living room armchair by the fire while her kittens slept on their bed near her feet. She'd had tea with Maxine twice that week, who was remarkably silent on what Emma should do about Jason. Maxine just kept telling Emma to 'follow her heart', but stopped short of telling her exactly what to do.

Emma tapped her pen against her open journal. After months of writing nearly every day, the journal was almost full.

She flipped back to the first page, to the two words she'd written just a few months earlier, months that somehow had seemed to span a lifetime.

What now?

Emma read the words over and over as she felt her eyelids get heavy, then fell asleep to the sounds of crackling wood.

Sometime later, she wasn't sure exactly how long, Emma woke to a dimmer fire after a vivid dream. The notebook had slid off her lap onto the ground, and she opened it to the last page before fumbling around the blanket in her lap to find her pen. She'd had a dream that reminded her of Jason, but she couldn't figure out exactly why. As she sat, watching the fire, she understood what she needed to do, how she needed to talk to Jason. It wasn't what the old Emma would do, or what a logical Emma would do.

It was what the new Emma, the woman she had been transforming into, would do.

So she wrote until she knew she had it right, and closed the notebook. She thought she wouldn't be able to fall asleep again, but within minutes, she did.

CHAPTER 33

Emma tapped the steering wheel with her fingers as she drove, and nearly turned around and drove home at every stoplight on her way through town. She had waited all day, pacing her small cabin, to finally convince herself to get in the car. She knew Jason was probably still out of town, but if she waited any longer, she thought she might chicken out. The drive reminded her of her trip from California to Montana – she was scared and headed towards the unknown, but she knew that there was no turning back. She had to keep going.

Emma found Jason's house without too much trouble, despite the snow making her trip longer than when she and Marcy visited for the barbeque. She pulled in the driveway and shut the engine off.

His house was even more beautiful covered in snow. The large porch that wrapped around most of the house, the wooden pillars that framed the entry steps. Everything showed Jason's care and personal touches, and as Emma's heart swelled when she admired Jason's work, she wondered how she had ever denied her feelings to herself. They seemed so obvious now.

Emma wrapped her scarf tightly around her neck, then grabbed the envelope and a roll of tape from her purse and left the warmth of her car. Jason had left lights on, and they threw an orange glow into the snow to light her path to his front door.

She walked slowly in case there was ice, and after what seemed like a year, she made it to his porch steps. Emma pulled off a long piece of tape and secured the envelope to the outside of Jason's door. She stared at his name in ink on the envelope, rubbing her fingers over the tape and wondering if she had gone completely insane. She could pull the envelope off the door, get back in her car, and go home. She could go back to work and, if Don hired her, find a way to be friends with Jason. She could forget all of this.

But Maxine's words came back to her in that moment, when she'd called as Emma was trying to get out of her rafting trip.

I'm not sitting here reminiscing about all the times I stayed behind, she'd said. *I'm thinking about all the times I didn't.*

Emma took a deep breath and pulled her hand away from the tape, leaving the envelope where it was. It would either confuse Jason or it wouldn't; it would either build something between them or not. But going backwards wasn't an option.

Emma walked away from the door and back down the steps. She opened the car door and kicked her boots against the side of the car to get the large chunks of snow off, and was about to step inside when she heard a door open behind her.

"Emma?"

Emma's heart picked up as she turned back towards Jason's house and saw him standing in his doorway.

"I thought you were out of town," she stammered.

Jason shook his head. "I just took some time off to get a few things done at home."

He stood with his hand on the inner doorknob, the door halfway open. From his position, he couldn't see the envelope Emma had taped to the outside of his door, but Emma could. The door divided the Jason who didn't know about her feelings from the one who could, and Emma stood frozen in the snow.

"Did I just hear you come up the porch?" he asked, and Emma nodded.

"I didn't hear you knock."

"I didn't knock," she mumbled.

"So you just walked up to my door and turned around?"

Emma debated her answer. She could say yes, and somehow try to steal her note back from Jason's door, since he still hadn't seen it. But then what?

"I left you something on your door," she said, pointing.

Jason peered around his door and pulled the envelope from the outside. As he started to open it, Emma thought about telling him to stop and wait until she'd left. But then she would just be waiting for his response, wondering what he thought. She had already delivered it, said what she needed to say. Her part was done, and while she couldn't control how he felt about it, she knew she needed to know.

Jason glanced at Emma as he unfolded the sheet of paper, and Emma nodded. As he began to read, Emma thought about the poem that had come to her late in the night. She'd read and re-read it a hundred times that day, wondering if it made sense, hoping Jason wouldn't laugh at it.

She watched Jason's face at the porch, shivering slightly in the cold as she blinked snowflakes from her eyelashes, and read along with him in her mind.

Last night, I dreamt I walked alone
In the fading light of the moon.
I passed a fence that had faded from time
And wind and weather and neglect.
But in the shelter of an oak
The paint shone bright and new,
Protected from the hazards of the earth.
I thought of you, when I saw the tree.
I thought of you,
And I thought of me.
And in the dream, I knew you.
You saw the bright parts of my fence
When all I saw was dim.
You saw me.
And as I dreamt, I hoped, like the oak,
That you'd stay nearby while I paint my life bright
And weather the storms with me.

Emma recited the poem twice to herself before Jason looked up. By the end of the second time, she knew she had made a mistake. Not only was she standing in his yard, slowly turning into a snowwoman as the snow continued to fall all around her, but the poem didn't make sense, and he wouldn't get it. Why couldn't she have just told Jason her feelings like a normal person and let him respond to that, rather than embarrassing herself?

Because this is who you are, a voice said from within her, and Emma nodded. This person who wrote poetry to explain her feelings and drove to a man's house in the middle of a snowstorm to deliver those feelings was exactly who Emma was. She was a woman who followed her heart.

Jason walked down the steps towards her with her poem, and her heart, in his hands. And Emma wondered if he knew that. He walked around her open car door and stood directly in front of her, staring down into her eyes. He was so close that Emma could feel the heat from his warm body, smell the smoke from the fire that must be burning inside his house.

After what felt like an hour, but was probably only a few seconds, Emma broke the silence.

"I'm not sure if it makes sense, but-"

Jason shook his head and ran a finger down Emma's cheek. The gesture was physically similar to how Blake had touched her just a few days earlier, but didn't feel at all the same.

"It makes sense," Jason whispered. He cupped Emma's face with his palm, and rubbed her cheek with his thumb.

"I take it this means you think I'm more than just a good photographer?" he said with a smile.

"I think you're a good everything," Emma whispered.

"I'm glad we're finally on the same page," Jason said, still smiling.

"Finally?" Emma asked, pulling her head back.

Jason sighed, pulling Emma's body towards him. She heard the poem and envelope rustle against her back, still in his hand, as he pulled her close.

"Emma, I've known you were special since that first time we danced. And I knew you were someone I wanted since we talked by the river. I was just hoping that eventually you would catch up."

Emma shook her head. She hadn't been ready for Jason when they talked at the river. She really hadn't been ready until she woke up the night before and wrote the poem for him. Even if part of her had thought he might possibly have feelings for her also, she wouldn't have believed they had existed for so long.

She didn't know what to say, but thankfully, Jason took the option away.

He leaned forward and gently tilted her face upwards with his hand, and put his mouth against hers in a kiss that warmed her from the inside out, despite the snow falling all around them.

CHAPTER 34

Emma stayed at Jason's house until Sunday evening, making sure to call Maxine to let her know where she was so her neighbor wouldn't worry herself into a heart attack. Maxine also agreed to check on Emma's kittens, under the condition that Emma would give her all the details when she returned home.

As Emma entered her cabin Sunday night, the events of the last day continued to wash over her, filling her heart with happiness. They'd stayed up late talking and kissing, and had finally fallen asleep on the couch in front of Jason's fire at nearly dawn. They'd made breakfast together, and Jason had taken Emma sledding on a hill behind his house. She didn't know if she was in pain from falling off the sled or from laughing too hard, but either way, she was too happy to care.

Emma played with her cats for a few minutes and fed them dinner, then looked through her curtains to see that Maxine's porch light was on, and the woman was likely waiting just inside the door. Emma was surprised she hadn't called yet, but she knew the call would come if she waited too long. She took a quick shower and changed clothes and was about to head over to Maxine's when she spotted her journal on the chair in the living room.

Emma sat in the chair and opened the book to a clean page. If she kept up this pace, she would need to ask for a new journal for Christmas.

What now? she wrote, and smiled.

Now, I live.

She closed the journal and set it on her chair, then wrapped herself up in her warmest coat and started the trek across the road to Maxine's. Emma had only just gotten back from Jason's, but her neighbor knew people all over town. She'd know what had happened soon enough, but Emma wanted to be the one to tell her. Maxine had helped Emma find the path to her heart; the least Emma could do was let her know she'd been right.

And hope it didn't go to her head.

ABOUT THE AUTHOR

Allison O'Shea is an author and blogger who lives
in Southern California with her husband and two
dogs.
Keep up to date with book releases and updates on
her website
www.allisonoshea.com
OR
Follow her on Facebook!

Made in the USA
Middletown, DE
04 February 2019